Forgotten Dreams

Moon Child 5

By Janet Lane-Walters

Print ISBNs
Amazon 978-0-2286-1001-4

BWL Publishing Inc.

Books we love to write ...
Authors around the world.

http://bwlpublishing.ca

Chapter 1

Chad Morgan leaned against the wall near the French doors leading to the garden of the ball room. The scent of June roses drifted on the breeze. A distant hum of traffic rumbled beneath the pop songs played by the band. Dark clouds played tag across the moon, carrying the promise of a coming storm. His thoughts approached another kind of storm, one burning in his gut.

Tonight was his to savor but the taste was sour. The celebration of his latest flick bored him. His muscles ached from the day's six hour workout to keep his body fit for another action adventure as the unbeatable Storm. The fourth of the franchise his agent and the studio hoped would never end had been released today.

Music blared, playing the latest tunes and of course, the series' theme song. Couples gyrated to the pounding beat. Women wearing glittering gowns and men in dark tuxes turned like fragments of glass in a kaleidoscope. He released a breath. Just another Hollywood party.

In a silent salute, Chad raised his glass and sipped. He welcomed the burn of rum and cola, his personal favorite written into the scripts as Storm's go-to drink. There were times when he really wanted a beer instead, but images must be maintained at all times and his kick-ass hero knew how to hold his liquor. He chuckled. Unlike his on screen persona, the glass he held contained his first and last alcohol of the night, a fact which of course no one else knew.

He watched a curvaceous blonde weave her way among the dancers, headed in his direction. She paused to lift a glass of champagne from a strolling waiter's tray. Her top shimmered beneath the lights. The low swoop of the neckline barely covered her nipples.

Chad sipped again. He should know her…Her name was Mindy, Mandy, Bimbo. Just one of the latest crop of aspiring starring ladies who managed to attend every important party. She glided closer.

"Hiding in plain sight?" Her husky whisper left him cold.

"Observing," he said.

"What do you see?"

He could answer with the truth but he wouldn't. Truth wasn't needed tonight. What he saw was false laughter, pretense and boring people. He looked past her. "The same thing I see at similar affairs. What's your pleasure?" He had an idea but he wanted to hear her ploy.

Her smile held a promise of activity he didn't want. She ran her hand along his arm. "I'm tired of secondary roles." She sucked in a deep breath and nearly exposed her nipples. "I hear there's another Storm movie being cast." Her fingers reached his shoulder. "You could let people see the chemistry between us. That's what your last leading lady did." She touched his lips. "I'm available."

"Did Cindy really do that? I never guessed." He fought the urge to laugh. Cindy's agent and his had orchestrated the romance that had only been in the papers, not in life.

He spotted the man he'd avoided all evening. Though he didn't want to speak to Gregson, the man's presence would chase this opportunistic female away. He stepped away. "Speak to your agent. Perhaps he can arrange a reading. Mine is on the way. He wants to talk."

She pulled a card from her cleavage. "Give me a call. I promise you won't be sorry."

Gregson arched an eyebrow. "A new conquest? Time for some promo ops and rumors."

Chad shook his head. "She wants to star in my next movie. Not happening."

His agent smiled. "Shame. You tempted?"

"Not interested. What's on your mind?"

"You need to sign the contracts for Storm five and six. They want to start filming in September."

Chad released the breath he held. "I need a break. I'm tired of being typecast." Before the four Storm films, there had been spots in three other action films. He pointed to a trio of babes headed in their direction. "I'm also tired of being a chick magnet."

Gregson scowled. "Goes with the territory. Think photo op."

"Not the kind of life I want anymore."

4

"What you want and what the studio demands shows you're not reading the right script. Do number five and six and they might give you a chance to do something else. It's the money, my friend. You opened in the top spot world wide this weekend. You need to keep doing what you do best."

Anger bubbled closer to the surface. Chad feared erupting like Old Faithful. "I'm sick of Storm. I'm tired of kicking ass. I'm fed up doing the same scene with slight variations again and again. I want to do Rob's book. You said the script was great."

Gregson's hand landed on Chad's shoulder. "Not your style. I've shopped the idea around. Had some interest but not with you in the lead role. Two more Storms and you'll be on your way to the bank with more millions. In two years we'll ask again."

In one long swallow, Chad finished the drink. He slapped the glass into Gregson's hand. "In two years I'll be dead from boredom." He stepped out into the dark night.

"Let me know when you're ready to toe the line," Gregson called. "You know you will."

Chad strode to his car. He wasn't toeing any line, not as Storm. Hollywood no longer held the glamour he'd embraced ten years ago when he'd arrived. He could have chosen a different road. His athletic abilities could have earned him a college scholarship but the acting virus had invaded his life. Four years of drama in high school and multiple roles in the local theater group had brought him here.

He'd followed that dream but there had been other dreams. Could he find them again? Smiling chocolate eyes in a lovely face surrounded by dark hair flashed in his thoughts. Had she found a dream different from the one they'd shared and he'd forgotten? He slid behind the wheel and drove to his large and lonely home behind stone walls. There were decisions to be made but not tonight. He would remember her...Emma.

In an unusual move, the moment he reached the house, he mixed a second rum and cola.

* * *

Emma Grassi strolled along the walk beside her evening's date. They reached the steps to the wide front porch of her large house. Light shone through the living room windows, showing that her sister remained downstairs.

At the door, Brady pulled her into his arms. His mouth covered hers. She felt nothing. Another nowhere evening. There'd been no man who had stirred her since...She pushed back all thoughts of the one who had sent her hormones racing.

She reached for the door. "Thanks for dinner and the movies."

"It was fun. I'll call." He bounded down the steps and walked to his car.

Emma sighed. What was wrong with her? She entered the house and slumped against the door. Brady, a successful attorney, single, attractive and nice hadn't stirred any feelings. Just like the dozen or so men she'd dated in the past ten years.

With a groan, she kicked off her heels and entered the living room. "Hi." She sat on the couch beside her sister. "This is a switch. Everything all right?"

Claire nodded. "For the first time since we left Kevin, Brian went to bed without a asking me to stay until he was asleep."

Emma studied her sister's face. The bruises from the beating had finally faded. "And you?"

"I'm great!" Claire's laughter brought memories of happier days. "I waited up for you to let you know Brian's starting at the Fern Lake Academy on Monday. Thanks for handling the tuition."

Emma leaned against the dark green cushions. "Glad to help."

"I wish I could do something for you. Since Mom died, you've been here for the four of us. You've a birthday soon. Would you like a party?"

"Manon and I have back to back birthdays and so do you. Rafe is a Cancer, too. We've something planned on the Fourth. You're invited to a Cancer birthday party."

"Don't remind me. Remember how you accused me of being selfish because ours are one day apart?"

Emma chuckled. "All because you wanted your own cake." She closed her eyes. Those days had changed in an instant when their mother died and she had stepped into those shoes. The youngest of the brood had recently graduated from college at the same time as she'd received her Master's as a nurse practitioner.

"The date?" Claire asked.

Emma shrugged. "Nothing special."

"Has there been anyone since high school?" Claire shook her head. "You've clung to your memories longer than I stayed with Kevin."

"Let's not go there."

"You should. Like that song from South Pacific, you need to wash that man right out of your life."

Emma rose. Did Claire think she hadn't tried and been stopped by the Cancer propensity for clinging to old things? "Good night." She walked to the door. How could she rid herself of the memories and yesteryear's dreams? Once she and Chad had planned to be together forever. He'd moved on and up. He's become a Hollywood star with women falling over him.

She undressed, showered and went to bed. Tomorrow she had hospital rounds to make and a day spent with her family. Monday meant another set of rounds and office hours.

On Monday morning a few minutes before nine, Emma parked behind the ranch house Manon had converted for the offices of her family practice. The door to the basement X-ray facility was open. Emma strode around to the front door and waved to Claire, now the office

8

manager. "I see Manon beat me."

Claire rolled her eyes. "She beat us all. Hospital patients okay?"

"Yes." The clock chimed the hour. "Time to begin."

Claire looked up. "Dr. Marshall's restless. She pulled all the charts for today. I think she'll deliver soon."

"Sure hope not. She has a month to go." She strode down the hall to her office, locked her purse in a desk drawer and slipped on a lab coat. She hurried to Manon's lair. Her partner paced around the room.

"Morning," Emma said.

Manon grinned. "And a good one to you." She rubbed her belly. "I pray this will end soon."

Emma laughed. "Not this soon. We're too busy."

"Agreed. Just becoming weary and feeling fat. How were rounds? Any problems?"

"Calm. All are responding to treatment. I'm waiting for the test results. Mrs. Bren is scheduled to leave when there's a bed available ad Fern Lake Nursing and Rehabilitation."

"That's great. Oh, John Reid will be by for lunch. His treat. I'm glad he decided to unretire for the duration. We won't have to worry about patient stealing."

Emma smiled. "I'll enjoy working with him again. He always treated nurses like they had brains."

Their new nursing assistant knocked on the

open door. "Patients are set for you." Karen said.

Manon beat Emma to the door. "To work. I'll take rooms two and four.'

"I'm on my way." Emma strode to room one.

She spent the morning examining and treating patients. Most of them had chosen Manon when she first arrived in town. Emma saw two new patients. One she referred to Manon. Always there were a few who insisted on a doctor rather than a practitioner.

At noon Dr. Reid arrived with two large insulated bags from Burger Bounty. While they ate, they talked about his hours and the list of patients with ongoing problems.

At one, he rose. "See you next Monday."

Manon laughed. "There's no need to start then. I've three weeks before I reach my due date."

The gray haired man grinned. "I can see the child has dropped. You also rub your stomach a lot."

"False labor. It's happened several times during the last week or so."

"We'll see." He saluted and strode away.

By four, Emma saw the last patient on her schedule. She went to her office to complete the records on the ones she'd seen. Her sister appeared in the doorway. "I'm leaving. Invoices have been sent to the billing service. So glad you and Manon decided to use her."

"So am I. My weekends used to be filled

with sending bills, sometimes two or three times for the same patient. I'll see you and Brian at the house."

Claire paused. "I need to thank Manon for recommending Brian to the Academy. He loves it there."

"I'm glad. Go so I can finish. See you at dinner." She returned to the computer.

Some time later, Manon strode into the office. "Ready to go."

"Just finished." She logged out, opened the drawer and removed her purse. "You okay?"

"Tired of sitting. Tired of waiting. When this child arrives and I'm back, I'll make sure you collect your debt."

"I'll collect."

"How?"

"I've considered two options. A cruise or a trip to California. I believe Dr. Reid could be persuaded to stay a bit longer."

"He sure seemed eager at lunch."

They walked out together. Emma watched her friend drive away. Hopefully all would go well. She hoped Dr. Reid's prediction was wrong. By the end of July, Manon would have the baby and by October the California trip would be on.

A laugh rose from her belly. Though a cruise sounded like fun, she favored the second option. California, here I come. She would visit the man starring in the memories that kept her tied to the past. *Drat my Cancer sun.* She and Manon had often talked about how hard getting rid of old things seemed to be hard.

Chad Morgan. His face floated in hr thoughts. In high school they'd been a couple. She had loved him and believed he loved her. He hadn't. Though she tried to forget the dreams, fantasies wove through her thoughts every night. She had to face him in person, in his own milieu, to put an end to the dream he'd forgotten and she had remembered.

From the tabloids and gossip shows. He'd changed from the boy she still remembered. Pictures accompanying the stories of his many affairs often caught her eye from the checkout counter at the grocery store, pictures and stories that shocked and angered her. Yet her dreams still clung like the fur of a white angora cat to a black dress.

* * *

After a restless night, Chad woke to the rumbling of thunder and the ping of rain hitting the windows. He dragged himself from the massive bed and planted his feet on the lush carpet. When he'd returned from the party, he'd had another rum and cola. Maybe two, an action in defiance of his usual routine of his usual single drink. He'd used the alcohol to escape the thinking of the past and the future.

He staggered to the bathroom and hit the shower. Water pelting from the various jets began the process of waking him. After showering and shaving, he dressed and ran down stairs to the kitchen to see what he could find for breakfast. The large room possessed every appliance a gourmet chef could desire. He laughed at the irony. All this for a man who could barely boil water. The kitchen had been his mother's dream. Her death two years ago had left the room barely used except for the single cup coffee maker, toaster and microwave or an occasional caterer. He'd grown used to eating in one of the area's many restaurants.

Chad popped a slice of bread into the toaster, poured a glass of orange juice and brewed a single cup of coffee. Now what?

As his thoughts churned, last night's anger and frustration popped up like the toast. His distaste for another go at Storm surfaced. He couldn't. Not without a reward at the end. How could he make his dream of other roles happen? Gregson couldn't or wouldn't fight unless he signed contracts for two more appearances as Storm, fighter for justice and lover of women. Two more films meant two more years in limbo. By then the studio would have ideas for at least one more. The treadmill stretched to infinity.

He could face his agent. The man had steered his career. He understood Chad's desire for more…but… . And there was always a but. Money. Chad pounded the table. He needed time. He needed space. He needed a friend. His thoughts turned to Rob. His friend's second book was due for release soon. A third was planned.

Lightning ripped across the sky. The

sudden burst of an idea struck. He would travel to Fern Lake and talk to Rob. The day they'd signed the contract for movie rights to the first book flashed into Chad's thoughts. He had vowed to make the movie and some how, he would.

He spread peanut butter on the toast. Fern Lake. People said you couldn't go home again. No one had ever said you couldn't visit. He bit into the toast and gulped some orange juice. After finishing, he sipped coffee and hit Gregson's number.

"Leaving for a few days. Need a quiet place to think." He disconnected and dashed upstairs to pack.

An hour later, he checked his duffle. He had enough casual clothes to last a week or longer. His wallet with his alternate identity rested in his pocket. He tucked the movie script for Rob's book, his real identity documents, and plenty of cash into the bag.

I'm out of here. In the garage he stowed his duffle in the Ferrari's trunk. He considered leaving his phone behind but he didn't know Rob's number or exactly where his friend lived. The Grantlan's mansion had been sold. He and Rob hadn't talked for months. During that time, Rob had married his high school sweetheart and adopted their niece.

After settling the phone in the dashboard holder, he programmed the GPS for Fern Lake. When he was closer to the town, he would call Rob for specific directions to his house.

As the garage door closed behind him, his phone chimed. He let the message go to voice mail. He had no desire to speak to Gregson before he had a solid plan. He drove to the interstate and dodged through traffic, heading east.

Two thousand eight hundred miles, give or take a few, according to the GPS, and he intended to make it well under the estimated trip time. He could have flown but people would know where he went and the press would have followed. Once he reached Rob's house, they would discuss the movie and how to produce the film.

Reaching Fern Lake was vital. During this trip he would only stop for gas, food and sleep.

So he left California and paid little attention to the scenery. As he drove, he considered his options. Change the Storm contract. Go to another studio. Find an independent film maker. Produce the film himself. That could be a way to use all the courses about films he'd taken over the years. Rob would help him decide. Though Chad owned the movie script, the book and final decision belonged to Rob.

On the third day of travel, somewhere in the Midwest, he stopped for gas and grub. After filling the tank, he pulled into the parking lot of a diner. He entered the classic building where he found a booth and studied the menu.

"Oh my god, it really is him," a shrill vice yelled.

A stampede of teens surrounded the booth.

One of the boys grinned. "Storm, my man, you doing a movie around here?"

"Could we be in it?" squealed a girl with pastel streaks in her dark hair.

Chad swallowed. How to get out of this? "Who the bloody devil is Storm?" He pulled a British accent from his community theater days.

"You're putting us on," A husky boy shouted. "We know you're not really Storm. You're Chad Morgan."

"You are so kick ass," a third boy said.

Chad reached into his pocket. "I fear you are mistaken." He flipped the wallet open and flashed his false license. "Ian Greve, at your service."

One by one the teens walked away. A waitress arrived and took his order. "You sure do look like him."

"I have heard everyone has a double."

When his meal arrived he dug in, finished, left a tip and paid the bill. Though he wanted to run, he sauntered to his car. That moment of identification had been closer than he wanted. He waved to the group of teens who stood outside the diner. "Cherrio."

"Nice wheels," one shouted.

On the afternoon of his third day of travel, exhaustion swamped him, though he wasn't far from his destination, exhaustion swamped him. He had to stop, find a room and sleep for at least eight hours or risk falling asleep at the wheel. He read the signs for the next exit and saw a sign for a motel five miles ahead. Moments later, he pulled into the parking lot and hoped there would be no repeat of the diner scene.

With cash and his alternate ID, he had no trouble registering. The desk clerk arched an eyebrow but made no comment. After a late lunch in the motel dining room, he went to his room and called Rob. According to the signs he figured he was a hundred and fifty miles from Fern Lake.

"Chad, where are you?" Rob asked. "The scandal sheets have you shacked up with your next starring actress."

Chad laughed. "Good to hear. Actually I'm on my way to your house. We need to talk about the movie. Just where are you living these days?"

"At the cabin."

Chad nearly laughed when he remembered the large structure Rob called a cabin. "Does the hideaway have a street address?"

"Just RDF on Mountain Road."

"Spell out the directions."

Chad wrote quickly as his friend spoke and read the directions back to him. "How accurate are the miles?"

"Very. I measured them one day. When you reach the gate, there's a box. You need to punch in these numbers." He recited them. "Since the trouble last year, the cabin has become a fortress." Chad read the numbers back. "See you tomorrow for lunch."

He stripped and sprawled on the bed. In seconds he slept. He didn't wake until nine the next morning. Though still tired, he showered and dressed. A hearty breakfast and a carafe of coffee energized him.

At the car, he read the directions into his phone and left. An hour later, he left the interstate and laughed. Forty miles to go.

Some miles later his voice came from the phone. Chad yawned until his eyes watered. "In three tenths of a mile turn right." He scanned the other side of the road and spotted the gate posts. In the distance a line of traffic approached with a slow moving truck in the lead. He had time to make the turn into the road leading to Rob's. He made his move and looked up.

"No," he shouted.

A pickup truck barreled from behind the line of cars and headed for the Ferrari. Chad hit the gas but not hard enough. The truck hit the rear of his car. Controlling the wheel was impossible. Though he tried to brake, his car slammed into the concrete gate post of the gate guarding the lane to Rob's house. For an instant Rob felt nothing. Then pain rolled through him. The sensation was so strong, he lost consciousness.

Chapter 2

After a Saturday morning of having breakfast with Claire and Brian and cleaning house, Emma picked up her bag. "I'm off to make rounds and visit Manon. See you this afternoon."

Brian grinned. "Mom and I are going to the playground near the school. Maybe some of my friends will be there."

"I hope they are." Her six year old nephew had settled into the summer program at the Academy and had made friends. "Have fun. We'll rent a movie and pop some corn this evening."

He clapped her hand. "Which one?"

Emma shrugged. "A surprise."

Claire winked. "Why rent one? You have a number starring you know who."

Emma glared. "They're not suitable for young eyes. I'm considering getting rid of them." That might be a good first step in the freeing herself from the past.

"Really?"

"Yes." In that instant she decided to stop yearning for what she would never have.

"Good to hear. Do you really intend to

forget him?"

Emma opened the kitchen door. "I believe I am."

"Good luck."

And she would need every iota of good fortune. She'd clung to a dream for ten long years. Losing this obsession would allow her to find love and a family. Though her resolve strengthened she felt a moment of sadness.

"Say hello and congrats to Manon," Claire called.

"Will do." After rounds she intended to visit her partner and see the son who, despite the fact that his official due date was a month away, had arrived early this morning.

She parked in the doctor's lot and hurried inside to visit the practice's four patients. For two she wrote discharge orders. On the others, she ordered new tests and consultations.

Rounds completed, she rode the elevator to the second floor and walked to the maternity unit. She tapped on the door of Manon's private room. Her friend reclined on the bed propped by pillows. Her husband lounged on a chair beside the bed.

"Congratulations to you both," Emma said. "So you managed to have your child born under our Sun sign."

"So we did," Rafe said. "And we'll be home in plenty of time for our mutual birthday party."

"We need to add Claire to the group," Emma said. "Hers is the day after mine."

"And Maria, Jay's new wife," Manon said.

Rafe rose. "I'm on my way home. Be in later."

"With food, I hope." Manon kissed him.

While they said goodbye, Emma stood at the clear sided crib to stare at the baby. Envy surged. She wanted one but before she could, she had to expunge her memories. "He's handsome."

Manon laughed. "Says a soon to be a doting aunt. Rafe Junior looks just like a baby."

"Guess you won the naming battle."

"Easily. Sit and visit."

"I'm happy for you." While she had four siblings and a young nephew, she wanted a child. Unfortunately, there was no special man in her life and she had no desire to become a single mother. All she had was a dream she must forget. She walked to the chair. "How do you feel?"

"Sore." Manon chuckled. "Lighter. Free. Tell me about the patients. Any potential problems?"

"We're down to two in-house. I'm asking OT to see Sally Lund. I think Dr. Reid should have a look at Mr. Palmo. I had to change his drugs again."

"Good thought about the consult." Manon yawned. "Six weeks before I can return to work. I'll owe you."

Emma nodded. "You will. I would like to take a trip in late September or early October."

"Where will you go?"

"California."

Manon frowned. "Why?"

"To put an end to feelings I've had for ages. Those regarding an old flame." Emma gulped a breath. "Do you know Fern Lake's most famous former resident lives there? We were an item in high school. I need to expunge my fantasies."

"Did you love him?"

Emma nodded. "Head over heels. I thought he felt the same. I waited for him to return. Didn't happen."

"Must have hurt." Manon touched her hand.

Emma nodded. She fought the rise of tears. "When his mother left town to live with him, she and I talked about my coming for a visit. I kept delaying to deal with my sib's teenage emotions. Then she died and for two years all I've seen or heard are tabloid stories. Yet like a fool I hoped. I need to tell him face to face how much I hurt."

"You're right. Years ago when I was told Rafe had died, I was furious. On the night of the prom, he'd run away and I didn't know why. Then I was told he died. When he returned I was hurt and angry. Slowly I learned the real story and we found each other again. Maybe seeing Chad will have the same result."

Emma shook her head. "Not possible. He has a different kind of life but I need to vent to him so I can move on."

"Then go for it. Wish I could tell you to leave now." She yawned again.

Emma rose. What her friend said made

sense. She must move away from childish dreams. "I'll stop by tomorrow when I make rounds and then visit you at home to deliver the gifts I haven't wrapped."

"Don't waste the paper. You know I would only tear paper to shreds."

Emma stepped into the hall. She could go home and make a sandwich but her stomach growled. Claire and Brian were having lunch out. She reached the ground floor and headed to the cafeteria. She assembled a salad and stopped for the chef to add thin slices of ham, turkey, cheese and eggs. After paying, she filled a large cup with iced tea and carried her lunch to a table near the window.

As she ate, a group of young nurses sat at the next table. Though she hadn't meant to listen, their loud excited voices caught her attention.

"I nearly went crazy when the ambulance brought him in," one nurse said.

"Why?" asked a second.

A third leaned forward. "We thought he was Chad Morgan."

The fourth laughed. "Why would a Hollywood hunk come to Fern Lake? We're not a tourist destination."

"Alas he isn't Storm." The first nurse sighed. "His name is Ian Greve. Still he has a face and bod to drool over."

"So what happened to him?"

"Car accident. He's responding but in pain. Keeps passing out and they can't give him anything for pain until the surgeon arrives."

Emma gulped her tea. She knew that name. Chad's middle name was Ian and his mother's maiden name was Greve. The nurses at the other table were too young to know Chad had been a track star and a leading actor in school and in community theater productions. She couldn't imagine any reason for him to come home. He never had before.

"I still wish I could be his nurse," the first young nurse said. "If he'll be here for weeks, there's a chance."

Emma finished her salad and carried her tray to the cleanup area. As she walked toward the exit, she paused. Curiosity stirred. If he was Chad, why was he in Fern Lake? She reversed direction and headed to the ER.

At the desk, she paused to speak to the nurse practitioner on duty. "I hear you have a new admit from a car accident."

Her friend looked up. "Ambulance chasing?"

Emma laughed. "If his name is Ian Greve, I may know him."

"Glad someone does." She frowned. "He's in pain and keeps talking about a pickup and a post. He also asks for someone called Rob. He's a real puzzle."

"Where is he?"

The second cubicle. Dr. Markham is on the way in. See if you can persuade him to sign a consent."

"I'll try."

Emma strode across the hall. She paused with her hand on the curtain. After gulping a breath, she slid the cloth aside. "Chad. Chad Morgan."

* * *

From a distance, someone called his name. He knew that voice. He'd heard her speak on the nights when he was without a female companion. He struggled to grasp the memories sweeping through his head like leaves captured by a tornado. Again the voice called his name. He fought to open eyelids sealed by glue. In the dim light he saw her. As his eyes focused her face took form. Emma was here. Was this a dream? With the force of a raging stream, pain rose from his toes to flood his body. A low groan morphed into a sharp cry. Someone's hand stroked his shoulder.

"You were in an accident." The voice, her voice, held a calm note of comfort.

He sucked in a breath. Panic engulfed him. "My legs. I can't move my legs." He pressed his hands against the mattress and attempted to sit. He had to see his legs. The fear of being unable to walk or enjoy physical activities thundered in his head.

"Calm down. Your legs are in splints to keep the bones in place. Both are fractured. A doctor is on the way. You need surgery."

"To amputate?" He grasped the sheet.

"No. They'll align the bones and apply

casts. For the left, they may need to put in a plate and screws."

Relief rippled through him. "Emma, what are you doing here?"

"You're in Fern Lake. I live here."

Fern Lake. Why? Realization broke through the curtain of pain. He'd come to Fern Lake to see Rob about the movie. His memories jelled. A voice. An urge to turn. A pickup. The impact. His bumper. The concrete pillar. The disjointed scenes flashed like bits of dust and vanished.

"Where is here?"

"Fern Lake General."

Chad's hands clenched as the level of pain soared. He couldn't remember experiencing this degree of pain. The edges of his vision blurred. He clung to consciousness.

A swishing sound. Chad clung to Emma's hand. A man wearing green scrubs entered. "Mr. Greve, I'm Dr. Markham."

Chad frowned. Who did the doctor think he was?

"Ian Greve," Emma said. "Remember your travel identity."

Chad swallowed. He understood but a dilemma had arisen. He needed to keep his identity hidden but his insurance wouldn't cover Ian Greve. He cleared his throat. "Grieve is my alias. I'm Chad Morgan. Is there a way to keep my identity a secret?"

The doctor frowned. "We could let your assumed name remain on the admission list even though using your real name wouldn't allow people to know anything more than you were a patient. There are rules to keep information from becoming public."

"You don't know the hyenas. They just keep coming." Chad released a held breath. "I'm sure they'll learn I'm here."

"I can alert Security and have a no visitor's warning in effect. Any exceptions?"

Chad's tense muscles uncoiled. "Rob Grantlan and Emma Grassi and anyone they vouch for."

"So noted." Dr. Markham stood beside the bed. "Here's the score. Fractured tibia and fibula both legs. The left is compound meaning bone piercing the skin. You were fortunate no major blood vessels were severed. You also have some spinal swelling from being bounced around a bit. A couple of bruises from the air bags. Yu may experience some numbness and tingling in your legs and feet. You'll need to sign a consent so we can take you to the OR."

Chad closed his eyes. "Is there a chance of permanent damage?"

"Maybe a residual limp. You'll have traction on the left leg until the skin heals and we're sure the bones are in place. Then a cast. You'll be immobile for a month to six weeks. Maybe longer."

Chad's hands clenched against the tsunami of pain washing through him. "Could...I...have...something...for pain." He hated to ask for anything stronger than an analgesic but he feared the scream building inside would escape.

"As soon as you sign the consent I'll arrange for something."

"Thank you."

Before Dr. Markham returned a nurse arrived with the form and an injection. The doctor wasn't far behind her and stood beside the bed. "Several questions."

The sharp edges of pain smoothed. Chad squeezed Emma's hand. "Ask away."

"Allergies?"

"None."

"Do you smoke?"

"Not any more."

Drug and alcohol use?"

"Drugs never," Chad said. "Alcohol. Never more than one rum and cola. Sometimes I'll have a beer or two."

"Good answers. We're taking you to surgery in a few minutes. Security is aware of you situation."

"Thank you."

The doctor left. Emma released his hand. "Good luck."

He reached for her. "Don't go. When I heard your voice, I thought I was dreaming. Stay until after the surgery. Call Rob for me."

"I can stay a bit and I'll make the call."

"Someone waiting for you?" *Husband, a significant other, a boyfriend?* He hoped no one.

She nodded. "My sister. After her divorce, Claire came home with her son to live with me."

As the team from transport wheeled Chad down the hall to the Operating Room, Emma walked beside the bed. She would stay until Rob arrived. The irony of the situation struck her. In her head, she'd devised many scenes when they met and she'd said her bit before walking away from the ghosts of the past. This meeting had never entered her thoughts. Anger and hurt had prevented her from imagining a time when she felt sorry for him. How odd to know he had no one who cared. She had never thought of a time when he would beg her to stay.

When they reached the wide doors into the operating area, she pressed his hand. "Good luck." The urge to kiss him shocked her. She stared at the closing doors, fighting the bubbling emotions she didn't want. She pulled out her cell phone. Claire received the first call. "I'm still at the hospital and will be here for several hours."

"Is Manon all right?" Claire asked. "What about the baby?"

"Both are great. My reason for staying is another matter. Think of a blast from the past. I'll fill you in later. I'll be home in time for dinner and the movie."

"Good enough.'

Though Emma felt sure Rob's phone was unlisted, she could slide through a side door. His wife was a nurse practitioner with a pediatric group and had become a consultant and a casual friend. Emma hit the number and smiled when she heard Andi's response.

"Emma, I'm not on call this weekend."

"I know. I need to speak to Rob about his friend who was supposed to arrive at your house today."

"Got you…Rob, there's news about Chad."

A moment later Emma heard Rob's deep voice. "How is he? I figured the mangled mess towed from my gate post was his. I called the hospital but they denied he was a patient. Is he…"

"Alive and battered. He uses a different name when traveling. He's at Fern Lake General and asked me to call you. He's headed to surgery. Both legs fractured. Tibia and fibula. The left was a compound."

She heard a bark of laughter. "Though it's not funny, he'll hate being inactive. Just who are you?"

"Emma Grassi, a friend of Chad's from high school."

"I remember you. Didn't you come to all his track meets?"

"I did." She released a sigh. She didn't want to dwell on the memories Rob's words had raised. "He asked me to stay until he's out of the OR."

"I'll join you. Glad it's Saturday and I don't work on weekends. See you in twenty."

Emma walked to the single cup coffee maker and prepared a cup. She thumbed through a magazine but her thoughts circled around what she needed to say to Chad. That meant confronting him and spewing all the pain his dropping her had caused. He'd moved beyond a high school romance. She had to do the same.

Memories of the track meets where he and Rob had competed rose. They'd been a matched pair. Though back then, though she and Rob had been friendly, they didn't move in the same circles.

Just as she finished the coffee, Rob entered. "Any news?"

"Nothing."

Rob sank onto one of the colorful plastic chairs. "Looks like Fern Lake will be a center for reporters and photographers."

"Maybe not. He's on the patient list as Ian Greve. Security knows. He also said the only visitors he wanted are you and me and anyone we vouch for."

Rob's brow wrinkled. "That's a change. The last time we were together he said every occasion was a promo op. Wonder what soured him."

Emma shrugged. "Before today, I hadn't seen him since he left for Hollywood. For many years we kept in touch. Then fame happened and he became tabloid fodder. Do you suppose he's in some kind of trouble?" She could think of several scenarios, especially when she recalled all the photos and stories she'd heard. Though she didn't want to believe the stories, she no longer knew him. Was there pregnancy, a child support issue, a broken contract, some

31

kind of sexual harassment suit facing him?

"We won't' know until he wakes." Rob tapped his fingers on the chair arm. "I know a way to keep the curious from ambushing him. My cousin is a partner in a security firm. He could provide guards."

"Better ask Chad first," Emma said. "As I remember, he never liked others making decisions for him."

"Bet that's changed. Having an agent means giving up a lot of control."

Just then, Dr. Markham stepped into the room. "Surgery is finished. Right leg casted. Left has a plate. He'll be in traction until the wound heals."

"He won't like that," Emma said.

"Doesn't have to like it, but he's got to deal with it." He turned to Rob. "Shame you no longer own the nursing home. He'll need some place like that until the bones heal. Then he'll need rehab."

"Though there's a good program there, I don't think he'd be happy with all the visitors and activities. How long will he be here?"

The surgeon shrugged. "Depends on when we can remove the traction and the wound heals so we can cast the leg. I'd say a week, maybe two. He said his insurance is platinum."

Rob chuckled. "With the way he bounces about in those movies, he needs good insurance. He does his own stunts."

Dr. Markham frowned. "He may need to find less strenuous roles."

"His spine?" Emma asked.

The doctor shook his head. "Spine is fine. A bit of whiplash, some bruising and strain from the crash. By Monday the stiffness should abate. He'll need a lift in his shoes and he may have a permanent limp." He turned and walked to the door.

Rob turned to Emma. "He might grow up and stop playing this Storm character."

"Doubtful." Emma didn't think her Leo friend could give up the attention he received.

"Let's visit him. Then I'll head home." Rob walked into the hall.

Emma strode beside him to the Recovery Room. Chad was one of two patients. She noted the intravenous in his arm and the smaller bag of antibiotics. The other arm had a second intravenous and a pump for self-administration of pain medication. She studied the traction and the leg in a sling. Finally, she looked at his face. He didn't appear to be someone who had been ill. His tanned skin held the glow of health. She noted Rob made the same inspection.

"Chad," Rob said.

Chad opened his eyes. "I feel like I've been dragged. Guess I'll be late to lunch."

""You're in good hands. Markham is the best."

"Thanks."

"You need to rest now." Rob clasped Chad's hand. "I'll be in tomorrow."

"Okay."

Emma changed places with Rob. "Surgery

went well. You'll be here for a week or two."
She touched Chad's fingers. "I'll check in
tomorrow. Rest."

As she turned away one of the nurses pulled
her aside. "Why is he wearing two arm bands
with different names?'

Emma winked. "HIPPA rules. You're not
to talk about him and if people start asking
questions, shrug. If they persist let Security
know. If you have to say something, ask them
why Chad Morgan would come to Fern Lake."

"Got you." The nurse's eyes widened. "I
bet there are people who would pay big bucks to
see him."

"Is losing your license worth the money?"

"I guess not.'

Emma walked away. She hoped Security
was alert. She stepped into the hall and nearly
did a U-turn. Janice Stone strode toward her.
Emma's shoulders stiffened. She didn't like the
blonde supervisor who thought every man in the
world desired her.

"Emma, a moment."

Though she wanted to retreat, Emma
halted. She hadn't worked with the other nurse
since Manon had returned and hired her as
office nurse and encouraged her to finish her
education. "Is there a problem?"

"Just wondering how well you know Chad
Morgan."

"We dated in high school but I'm here to
visit Ian Greve."

Sandra laughed. "I'm the supervisor and

must know all about our patients. I'm aware of the false name."

Emma drew a deep breath. "Then you know the reason for the secrecy."

"I do. Don't worry. I won't tell."

Emma turned away. *Good luck, Chad.* Though Janice was older than the young actresses Chad preferred, she did fit his type. Blonde, beautiful and bold. Why did that make her gut curdle? Her hands clenched. She wouldn't be drawn back into the dream of being with Chad. She had to look at this encounter as a way to end her yearning for him.

As she left the hospital a drizzle began and soon changed into a steady rainfall. Emma arrived home just before her sister and nephew. She hurried upstairs to change into shorts and a tee shirt. The rain continued and the air steamed. When she reached the kitchen, Brian ran to her. "We had fun at the park. I swung so high I nearly touched the sky."

Emma ruffled his hair. "Sounds like fun."

His dark eyes shone. "Did you have fun, too?"

"A long but interesting day." Emma helped her sister unload the insulated bag from Burger Bounty. "Manon's doing great and the baby is handsome."

"You said you were staying and you would tell me why later."

"I identified a car accident victim."

Claire waved to her son. "Wash your hands and face." She pulled catsup from the fridge.

"Someone we know?"

"Emma nodded. "Chad.""

"As in Fern Lake's claim to fame? Action hero, Storm, Hollywood's darling? Is he here to make a movie?"

"A movie," Brad shouted. "Is he coming to the house?"

Emma shook her head. "He's in the hospital."

Brian bounced on his chair. "Wait 'til I tell my friends my Mom and aunt know a movie star."

Emma touched his shoulder. "You can't tell anyone he's here."

"Why not?"

"He was hurt and he needs quiet to get better so he doesn't want people bothering him."

Brian sighed. "Could I meet him? I promise not to tell."

"Someday." Though she saw disappointment in his eyes, she knew he wouldn't say anything. She vowed she would find a way for him to meet Chad.

After dinner, Emma popped corn. They went to the living room to watch a movie. As the credits rolled, Brian yawned. Claire lifted him from the couch. "Bed."

"Night, Aunt Emma."

"Happy dreams."

When Claire returned, she poured two glasses of wine and handed one to Emma. "So tell me about him."

Emma sipped. "Seeing him was a shock.

He's as good-looking as he was years ago. More muscular. Seeing him in person sent me back to those old dreams. I must really cast them out."

"So why did you stay?"

"He asked me and I felt sorry for him. I called Rob Grantlan to let him know about the accident and surgery. Chad was on the way to Rob's house." She set her glass on the end table. "Janice Stone was on her way to vamp him. She's his type."

"Did that bother you? I understand that woman has her eyes on every man she sees. Will she add another notch on her bedpost?"

Emma shrugged. "I'm sure he can handle her."

"Do you wonder if you and he could regain what you've lost?"

Emma finished her wine. "Too late for that." She rose. "I'm for bed. See you in the morning."

Thoughts of Chad followed her to sleep. Instead of California, she had to face him here. But not yet.

Chapter 3

Chad groaned and opened his eyes. Green curtains covered both sides and the front of his room. What was behind the side curtains? He turned his head and saw a large plastic bag with a tube leading to his arm. He blinked to focus on the dim light. He stared at his left leg suspended in a sling. Thin pieces of metal protruded from the skin. He could see ropes that must be attached to something.

Where was he and why was he in a bed with sides? Storm never ended up in a hospital. This wasn't a movie role then, something had happened to him. What?

With the force of a flash flood breaking through a dam, memories of the wreck arose. Excruciating pain and...Emma. Rob had also appeared in the dream. He had to move and escape to learn where he was. He pressed his hands against the pillow but he couldn't sit or move his legs.

Waves of pain flowed from his toes. "Help." Was that wimpy voice his? He swallowed and shouted again, this time with more force.

What was this place? A torture chamber?

Was this part of a script for a movie? If so, why did the pain escalate like a rocket headed to the stars?

The front curtain slid open. A young woman wearing blue scrubs entered. "Ian, how can I help you?"

For a moment he opened his mouth to correct her. Though his middle name was Ian, few people knew. What had he done? "Water," he croaked.

She filled a plastic glass and bent a paper straw before holding the glass so he could drink. "Are you having much pain?"

"Yes."

She placed a button in his hand. "On a scale of one to ten, with one being the lowest, how would you rate your pain?"

"Ten and soaring."

"This button connects to a pump. If you click it, you'll receive a dose of pain medication. What you must remember is to use the pump sparingly."

He pressed the button. Something heated flowed through his vein. "Am I in the hospital?"

She nodded. "Fern Lake General."

"What day of the week?"

"Sunday. Six AM."

"Is the doctor around?"

"Dr. Markham will be in later. If you need a doctor there's one on duty here."

He shook his head and closed his eyes so his concern wouldn't show. "I have a dozen questions Dr. Markham can answer. I'll wait."

The pain medication had begun to dull the edges of the agony. "Other than my legs, what's the damage?"

"A lot of bruises from the airbag and the seatbelt."

"My spine?"

"Just some whiplash damage." She winked. "I fear your car is totaled."

"I'm sure. Anyone else hurt?"

"Haven't heard of anything major. You were the only person admitted."

She left the cubicle. Chad dozed off. At least there wasn't an injection with a foot long needle this time.

A second nurse entered the area. "Would you like a glass of juice? I can also scrounge up some yogurt. Breakfast isn't until eight."

Chad shook his head. "I'll wait."

Before the meal arrived, he woke to see a machine wheeled to the bedside. An X-ray technician positioned a plate to take shots of his left leg. "Is it all right?" Chad asked.

"Won't know until the doctor has a look." The machine rolled away.

Chad considered using the medication pump but breakfast arrived. The nurse raised the head of the bed so he could eat. He uncovered the items on the tray. Oatmeal. He hadn't eaten that since he was a child. Rubbery scrambled eggs, dry toast, milk, orange juice and tea. Tea when all he craved was coffee. Hunger drove him to eat while thinking about his usual morning meal. Fluffy omelets, slices of ham or sausage or bacon. Waffles or pancakes. Cups of steaming coffee.

He had just finished the tasteless meal when the stacked blonde who had approached his bedside yesterday entered and closed the curtains. She glided to the bedside. "I hope you're feeling better."

Chad shrugged. "About the same."

She slid her hand along his arms. "If there's anything more you need, just ask the nurses to page Janice Stone. You'll soon be transferred to a private room."

Her gaze roamed from his chest to his groin. Chad's hands clenched. She checked him the way a butcher eyed a slab of beef. "I'm fine."

"I could make you feel better." She ran her tongue over her lower lip. "I know who you are but trust me to keep your secret."

Chad swallowed the words he wanted to say. She had nothing to offer him but sex. "I get you but no."

"I'll return when you're in your room. I'll bring you food. You'll be able to have visitors."

He shook his head. "There are only two names on the list. Security has them. If any are added, I will do the adding."

"You'll be so lonely." She stroked his arm. "I know ways to end your loneliness."

Something in her manner made him fear she would betray his presence if he didn't leap on her offer. Not happening. He couldn't tell her to get lost. He couldn't tell her she left him cold.

His jaw clenched. He hated the reputation he had developed during the past few years.

The curtain blocking the cubicle from view slid open. Chad didn't care who had arrived. He'd been saved. Emma entered. The look on her face troubled him but the sight of her brought a rapid response. The blonde moved away.

Emma smiled. "Janice, are you supervisor for the entire weekend. Isn't that unusual?"

Janice nodded. "Regina had an emergency with one of her kids so I volunteered." She turned to Chad. ""Since your medical attendant is here, I'll go and return later."

Chad prayed this was a promise she wouldn't keep. Emma's glare gave him hope.

Emma moved closer to the bedside. "You're looking better."

"I feel like a bulldozer flattened me. They're moving me to a private room today. I worry about being invaded there."

"You're right to worry. There are photographers and reporters outside looking for a story."

Chad shook his head. "I hope Security is tight here. I won't see anyone but you and Rob."

"Unless you hire private nurses, there will be people entering your room. The nurses, care aides and other personnel."

"I know. I mean outsiders."

"How will you prevent them? I imagine someone working here could be bribed to sneak someone in."

"I'll find a way."

"I'm not sure how often I can visit. My partner just had a baby. Office hours will be hectic but I'll try to pop in after rounds."

He closed his eyes. "You're abandoning me?" He hated the whine in his voice.

She grasped the side rail. Her knuckles whitened. "I understand you're used to attention from women who see you as a strong, virile and sexy man. Are you afraid of your fans seeing you as helpless?"

She spoke a truth he didn't want to admit. He chewed on his lower lip. "Probably."

"Sorry to hear that." She stepped back. "I can't be your constant companion. I have a life."

He stared at his hands. "Is this about our past?" When she nodded, shame washed through him. In his rush to fame he'd forgotten what she'd meant to him. "Emma."

"I don't want to discuss the past."

"I wish I'd been a better friend."

She backed toward the door. "I'll visit when I can."

"Emma." He wanted to leap from the bed and grab her to keep her from leaving. The curtain closed.

* * *

Though she heard Chad call her name and caught the hint of yearning in his voice, she continued to hurry away. The past lay like a stone wall between them. Hollywood, screaming fans and fawning women. Everything she'd read and heard shouted his life of being stage front. Her life was here and the partnership with Manon.

Outside ICU, she halted and drew a deep breath to stem remembrances of what had been. They'd been young and in love. The future had been a dream. She couldn't return to those days. Moving forward meant having no dreams.

Back to work. Finish rounds. Go home and spend time with Claire and Brian. She had her life. He had his. As she left the hospital, dark clouds released a steady stream of rain, rather like the tears she refused to shed.

* * *

Chad slumped against the pillows. Her final words echoed like a shout in the mountains reverberating from peak to peak. Was the past all they had? Was there a way to find a future? Was it too late to make amends? Seeing her again had stoked the feelings he'd forgotten. Years ago, he had been captivated by the glitz and glamour. He'd found an agent who had used photo ops to gain Chad the role of Storm. He couldn't change the past. His fears coiled into a ball. Would Emma avoid him? He vowed to find a way to change the present.

A short time later, Dr. Markham entered the cubicle. "X-rays show the bones are aligned correctly. You'll be transferred to a private room we usually keep for isolation though that won't deter the determined."

"How long will I be here?"

"At least ten days to two weeks. Depends on how well you heal. Once you have a full cast on both legs, you need to go somewhere where you have help with your daily care until the casts are off. Be about four to six weeks."

Chad groaned. "Then what?"

"Rehab somewhere. Physical therapy. Maybe Occupational Therapy." Dr. Markham paused. "A bit of advice. Consider a career change. The roles you currently play bring a chance of further damage."

Chad nodded. "Write a letter saying this is the case and I'll thank you. I would happily never play Storm again."

"I'll see one is sent to you."

Chad leaned back. His grin threatened to break his jaw. Wait until Gregson hears this news. Shame he didn't have his phone so the doctor could make the announcement.

Not long after Dr. Markham left, a transport team arrived and wheeled Chad's bed to the promised private room on the fourth floor. They entered the anteroom. A long table held a sink with a place to work. A linen hamper was nested beneath the table. Inside the spacious room, the bed faced the large window. He watched rain pelting the glass.

Moments later Rob and another man followed the nurse inside. While she checked the traction and did a quick assessment, the pair sat on the chairs.

After she left, Rob looked up. "Don't know if you remember my cousin. Simon is a partner in a security firm."

Chad appraised the other man. "High school. Football. Two years behind me."

"You've got it."

"Why didn't you go to the Academy?" Chad asked.

Simon laughed. "I'm the poor relative. Rob said you need a protective detail to keep unwanted visitors from invading your space."

"I sure do. I'll be here maybe two weeks. Then who knows where I'll go."

"I've an idea but I have to see if it will work." Rob opened an insulated bag. "They're probably chasing your lunch down so I figured a burger would be a treat."

"From the Bounty?"

"Where else?"

While Chad devoured the burger and huge fries, Simon discussed a protection detail. "Are you concerned about the cost?"

"I'm good for a chunk of cash, especially if I can retrieve my duffle. There's cash, my credit cards and check book."

"You'll need three men for eight hour shifts."

Rob leaned forward. "Even nights?"

"The secret is out," Simon said.

Chad nodded. "The rain's keeping them from clustering outside but the sun will shine tomorrow."

"You are so right," Simon said. "Security

ejected two men trying to invade ICU. They had cameras. Security will welcome the help."

Rob pulled a phone from his pocket. "Your duffle is at my house." He tossed Chad a phone. "You were lucky no one found your stash. Why so much cash?"

"I didn't want to use credit cards," Chad said. "Use them once and paparazzi are on your trail. I wanted to escape for awhile."

"You found an interesting way to do that," Simon said.

Chad chuckled. "You are so right."

When the two men left, Chad relaxed. Protection had been arranged. At four o'clock, Simon would arrive with the first of his guards. Chad reached for his phone and hit voice mail. His agent had called at least ten times a day. After hearing the first, he deleted all but the last. Gregson had heard about the accident and would come to Fern Lake to talk about the accident and the studio's new version of the fifth Storm movie.

Chad groaned. He needed to find a safe refuge for his remaining time and a way to avoid his agent until his future plans were set.

* * *

On Monday morning after a restless night, Emma overslept. She dressed quickly and grabbed a slice of toast and a mug of coffee to eat on the way to the hospital for rounds. There wasn't time to see Chad. The relief she felt brought a sigh. All night dreams had awakened her. Frustration dreams where she couldn't move or ones where she ran toward a goal ever out of reach. She gripped the steering wheel. What did he expect from her? She dare not ask.

Her second in-patient was in ICU. She read the notes and agreed with the neurologist to have the elderly man transferred to a medical unit and await nursing home placement.

A quick scan of the charts showed Chad had been transferred. None of the nurses on duty knew or wouldn't say where Ian Greve was located. She had no time to visit Security. She finished rounds and drove to the office.

Her forehead wrinkled. Why the frustration? Not knowing where he was had prevented a visit. Even though she shouldn't, she wanted to see him. Why these mixed feelings?

When she entered the converted ranch house, she saw two patients in the waiting room. She waved and paused at the desk.

Claire looked up. "You were a bit rushed this morning. I left a container of yogurt on your desk. The radiologist is in this morning in case you have anyone who needs one."

Emma shook her head. Manon had rented the large basement of the house to a radiologist who came in every Monday, Wednesday and Friday. "I don't think so." She hurried to her office and opened the container. Before she finished, Karen popped into the room.

"Your patients are waiting," the nursing

48

assistant said. "Dr. Reid has already begun."

"Which rooms are mine?"

"Two and four. If you need me, call."

Emma scraped the yogurt container and donned a lab coat. She strode to the door to begin her day.

Her first two patients arrived for their yearly physicals. She wrote orders for lab work. For the next three, she checked blood pressures, reordered meds and lectured on diets for hypertension. A teen with a red raw throat needed a throat culture. The scarlet tissues shouted strep. Strep required antibiotics but she wouldn't order them before the culture results came in. Antibiotics had no effect on a viral infection.

"I'll have the results of the culture later today and will call in a prescription if needed." She hoped this wasn't the first of a cluster of strep infections. She entered the small lab and began the culture. Doing them on side rather than sending them to a lab saved time.

By the time lunch arrived her sleepless night brought yawns and the desire for a nap. Claire arrived with salads and heroes from a nearby deli. While they ate, she, Dr. Reid and Karen talked about the patients they'd seen.

"I recommend you start the young man on antibiotics now," Dr. Reid said.

"But there's a chance this is viral," Emma said. "I'll check the culture before I leave."

He nodded. "How sure are you about your diagnosis?"

"Maybe ninety percent."

"You need to trust your gut." He smiled. "That will take time."

After he left to do notes on his morning patients, Emma called Manon. "How are you and Junior doing?"

Manon chuckled. 'Getting used to each other. He woke every three hours so my sleep was jumbled."

"Mine, too."

"Why?"

"Chad Morgan is in town. Actually at General under an assumed name."

"Really. Are you going to see him?"

"I did. Yesterday after I visited you." She sighed.

"Will you see him again?"

"I don't know. There's a lot of the past to solve." Karen waved to her. "Got to go. Patients await."

At four Emma saw the last patient for the day. Dr. Reid had left at three. She checked the culture under the microscope and called the prescription to the pharmacy. She walked down to see the radiologist. "There'll be three for you on Friday." She handed him the forms. "If you need to change the times, call them."

He checked his book and filled in the names. "Looks good."

Emma returned to her office and completed her records for the day. As the last to leave, she checked the doors.

When she arrived home, Claire turned from

the slow cooker where she was dishing out the chicken she had cooked all day. Emma drained the noodles and vegetables. Brian put the silverware on the table. After dinner, Claire and Emma cleaned the kitchen while Brian chattered about his day.

"Are you going to see you know who?" Claire asked.

Emma shrugged. "I'm not sure I should. Not knowing where he's been transferred to might be for the best."

"Go. You need to tell him how you feel. And how you wasted years waiting for him. When I think of my time wasted waiting for Kevin to change, I want to scream. I believe you should take this chance."

"You're right." Emma ran upstairs to her bedroom, showered and changed into jeans and a sleeveless bright blue tunic. "Wish me luck."

"I do and also guts."

She drove to the hospital and parked. Several men and women with cameras and mikes stood near the entrance. A woman thrust a mike in Emma's face. "What can you tell me about Chad Morgan?"

"Who?" Emma continued past. She heard the woman ask another visitor the same question.

Once inside, she walked to the Security office and tapped on the door. The guard looked up. "How can I help you?"

"I'm here to see Chad Morgan. I'm Emma Grassi. I'm on the list."

"Driver's license."

She handed it to him. He looked from the picture to her. "401 East. He has a guard there."

"Thanks."

When Emma reached the room, she paused in the anteroom and faced the guard. "I'm Emma Grassi." She offered her driver's license.

He lifted a camera and snapped Emma's picture. "For our use."

Emma walked into the inner room. Chad's bed faced the huge window. She approached the bed. "How do you feel?"

"Helpless. Bored. I'm stuck in this bed until the wound heals and a cast is in place." He groaned.

Emma nearly laughed. "You're alive. Your bones will heal. You'll be back to Hollywood and your life there."

"Maybe. You know how I hate being tied down."

She shook her head. "I really don't know you any more."

"That's my fault. Emma…"

From the anteroom, she heard Sandra's throaty voice. "I'm the supervisor and must be sure all the patients on the unit have the best care."

Emma saw the look on Chad's face. "You can't run."

"Don't I know it."

Sandra pushed the door open. When she saw Emma, she halted. "What are you doing here?"

Before Emma had a chance to speak, Chad grasped her hand. "Emma's an old friend. She's one of the people on my list. We're catching up on what's been happening since the last time we were together."

Emma wanted to laugh at the expression on Sandra's face. She also wanted to push the other woman out the door. She tensed. Those kind of thoughts had to end.

Sandra wheeled. "I'll be back and we can discuss the matter we talked about before." She shut the door with a loud click.

Chad growled. "Spare me from needy, greedy women."

"Ignore her. Insult her. Tell her you're taken. That might stop her."

"Wish I could say that."

Emma shook her head. He could have been taken but he hadn't cared enough to keep in touch.

"Could I add her to the list of photographers and reporters?"

"You could but she's a supervisor and is responsible for your care. Also when she has a man in her sights, she'll keep trying."

"I won't be here forever. I'm counting the days."

Emma pulled her hand free from his grasp. She hated the simmering sensations rolling form his touch. "What has the doctor told you?"

"Spine is fine. I'll be here until the stitches are out and the cast is a full one. Then I leave but I have no idea where I'll go. Home, I suppose but I need to talk to Rob. We have plans to make."

"About what?"

"Turning Rob's first book into a movie with me as the lead."

Emma frowned. "I've read the book. Is that your kind of role? You've done no straight drama roles in Hollywood."

A dozen emotions flashed on his face. "I'm tired of fights and chases. Remember the community theater? And that in the high school I played different characters? The studio wants me to do Storm two more times. The doctor thinks that's a bad idea."

Emma stared at her hands. How could he give up his role as Storm when he was paid millions for each film? As a teen he'd hated how hard his mother had worked. Money had been important to him.

"Do you really want to stay in Fern Lake?"

He shrugged. "If I could find a place where I wouldn't have to face photo ops and interviews. Besides, at home my bedroom is on the second floor." He tugged her closer.

Though Emma knew she should back away, she couldn't move. Her body felt distanced from her mind. The movement of his fingers on her hand brought a rush of heat. Throbbing began low in her belly. Her nipples peaked. Her heart rate accelerated. When his lips brushed hers she fought to control her desire to surrender.

A rapping at the door allowed her to step back. Chad growled. "This isn't finished."

Rob paused in the doorway. "Sorry."

Emma smiled. "I was just leaving. How is your niece?"

"Growing and chattering."

Emma walked to the door. She heard Rob's suggestion. "Why not come to my house when you leave?"

She turned. "I'll see you tomorrow after rounds."

Rob laughed. "Don't let those vultures outside find out you know Chad. The secret is out."

"I saw them when I came in."

Chad growled. "I'll find a way to avoid them." He paused. "When you come tomorrow we have a lot to talk about."

"There won't be time."

As she drove home she fought to dampen the pulsing need she'd felt during the kiss. She couldn't allow resurging dreams to fill her thoughts. Too much of her life belonged to Fern Lake. The practice, her home, her family. To leave and be a stranger among people who weren't her kind caused a chill despite the warm day. She hoped Chad would listen when she told him there would be nothing in the future between them.

Chapter 4

Rob settled in the chair beside the bed. "Sorry I chased your visitor away." He arched a brow. "Were you and Emma talking about the past?"

Chad drew a deep breath. "We were." For a moment he savored the kiss. "I'm glad she promised to come back. I blew my chances with her years ago by letting fame and flattery go to my head. I wish I'd been a better friend."

Rob nodded. "Years ago, I did a number on Andi. I hurt her more than I imagined. She finally forgave me. Having to share custody of Tammy helped."

"We've nothing to bring us together. I'm scrambling to find something."

"There's always hope."

"If I can keep her around long enough for me to grovel. She said she'll visit after rounds tomorrow. Her coming this evening surprised me." He stared at the window. "I can't wait to escape this place. I just need to find a place where I can see her."

"Come to the cabin," Rob said.

Cabin was an oxymoron for the spacious additions to the log cabin. "Are you sure? I'm kind of helpless. What does Andi think of your idea?"

"She's on board and is researching equipment." Rob pointed to the pull bar above the bed. "With someone to hold your legs while you flex your muscles, you can be wheelchair ready. There are plenty of bedrooms."

"I'll consider the possibility. Won't my presence interfere with your writing schedule?"

"You'll be no trouble." Rob shook his head. "There's a nanny for Tammy. I work from nine to noon. Break for lunch and back from one to three." He laughed. "The mite will enjoy having another man to enchant."

Perhaps this would work. "Let me look into the Rehab place first." Being at Rob's would give them time to discuss the movie. "I'll be here for awhile so we have time to work out a plan."

Rob rose. "You're coming. I'll start arranging things."

"If you have my duffle, there's a script for your book in there." He groaned. "I need something to occupy my time. There's not much on TV during the day. A book or two would be great."

"That can be arranged. Tonight's dinner will be delivered. Food from Tony's. There'll be enough for you and your guard."

"My stomach thanks you."

Rob walked to the window. "You'll have a great view of the fireworks on the Fourth."

Chad's brow wrinkled. Today was the

second. His mind wandered to other July Fourths in Fern Lake. The town's display had always been wonderful. He and Emma had sat on her dad's front porch to watch. She had allowed him to steal kisses between the bursts of color. Could he persuade her to watch them with him this year?

At five thirty, after sending the hospital dinner away, Chad waited for the Italian feast. He'd only eaten at the local five star restaurant once as a guest of Emma's father. The owner had been introduced as an uncle. Chad salivated as he remembered the great food.

From the anteroom, he heard a commotion. He turned to look through the glass panel of the door. His guard tried to accept the bags a delivery person held. Three men with cameras attempted to push past.

One photographer oozed into the room. Chad pulled the sheet to cover his head. A flash went off. More flashes exploded. Several Security men from the hospital arrived and herded the paparazzi away.

The guard carried the large bags into the room. "Sorry about that."

"I'm amazed this hadn't happened before. I wonder who leaked the news about my location."

"Could be anyone of a thousand," Jeff said. "I saved our meal."

"Let's see what they sent. Don't feel bad about the breach. Once they invaded my house and caught me in the shower. Thank heavens I was alone and behind semi-opaque glass. I had to build an electrified wall around the property."

"Must be a pain having no privacy."

"You've got that." As Jeff passed the containers, Chad opened them and inhaled the garlicky aroma. "There's enough food to feed a dozen. We'll make our choices and make a plate for the night man. We'll give the rest to the nurses."

"Sounds good."

Chad laughed. "Why a dozen cannoli?"

"I have no idea. The nurses will love them.

The rest of the evening was spent watching TV and wondering when the pins would be removed so he could leave the bed.

The next morning brought a visit from a physical therapist and some upper body exercises. Chad was able to use the dangling triangular bar to lift while his sheets were being changed. He also learned some exercises for his right leg.

When Dr. Markham visited, Chad learned the left leg cast would extend above his knee while the right didn't. This news made him growl but there was no choice.

As he drifted to sleep, he thought about Emma. Would she stop by tomorrow or not? Was not visiting today deliberate, or had she just been too busy? Was she avoiding him? That thought bothered him. Since the kiss, he'd wanted more.

He woke to voices. "Then I won't bother him. Let him know I stopped by."

59

"Emma, I'm awake." He rubbed his eyes and elevated the head of the bed.

Emma stepped into the room and paused at the foot of the bed. "How are you feeling?"

"Better now you're here. Missed you yesterday."

"Yesterday was crazy. I was held up doing a physical on a new patient and was late for office hours."

"Surely you're off today."

"After rounds I am."

"Why don't you come back this evening and watch the fireworks with me? I have a great view."

She walked to the window and then returned to the bedside. Chad waited for her answer. "Sorry, my day is booked."

He clasped her hands. "Surely not for the entire day."

"Afraid so. After I go home, Claire and I are taking Brian to the fair. Can't wait to watch him on the rides."

He grinned. "You going to ride the Ferris wheel?"

"Never."

Chad knew why. She and her sister had been stuck at the top of a Ferris wheel when it had broken down. Hours had passed before the repair allowed them to reach the ground.

He squeezed her hand. "That's only part of your day."

"We're going to a barbeque at my partner's house after. It's a Cancer birthday celebration.

Then it's off to watch the fireworks."

His spirits thudded to the ground. "Are you avoiding me?"

She met his gaze. "What we had can never come again. You should realize that."

He scowled. "I don't believe you. I'm willing to tell you what happened."

She shook her head. "I know what happened."

Damn, Chad thought. He would show her the old magic remained. He released her hand and pulled her against his chest. He captured her mouth. The rise of desire began. His tongue slid along her lips with teasing touches, He ran a hand over her back. In an instant, her lips parted as his tongue slid into her mouth, tasting.

When the need for a breath arrived, he freed her mouth. "Tell me you felt nothing."

She backed away. "I can't. Thinking about a future would be a dumb move on my part. I want you but I don't need you. I can never forget you dropped me for affair after affair. You only want me because for a short time I'm here and so are you." She opened the door.

Chad stared at the closing door. He slumped against the pillows. He'd been a fool. When Gregson had taken over his career goals, Emma had been pigeon holed for later. He's always believed when the time was right, she would be there. He wanted to shout, to slam his fist against the wall…to cry.

* * *

Emma wanted to run but she walked casually from Chad's room. What was wrong with her? The kiss had brought her old feelings for him to the surface. She had vowed not to fall for his line or his kisses. She wasn't sure why she had stopped to see him this morning.

Liar! The word revolved in her thoughts. Visiting him had been a dumb move. As long as being around him sent desire soaring, she couldn't move forward. Oh, for indifference!

She left the hospital and drove home. Brian danced around the porch. "Hurry, Aunt Emma. We're going to the fair."

She laughed. "So we are." She dashed upstairs and changed into shorts and a top.

Claire met her at the foot of the stairs. "He's so excited."

"So I see. He needs to have fun."

"You're right. Until we left Kevin, Brian was on edge all the time. I so blame myself, especially when Kevin slammed him into a wall."

"That's over." Emma slung her small bag across her body.

Fifteen minutes later they reached the fair grounds. Brian rode a miniature rollercoaster, circling cars and airplanes. He ran to the merry-go-round. Emma joined him on a horse and pretended to race him.

After the ride finished, they walked and paused to let Brian play a few games. He carried a stuffed cat he'd won in the fish pond. They stopped at the hot dog truck usually found near the lake and ordered their lunch.

Claire took a bite of her chili dog. "These are wonderful. I missed them."

"We'll go to the lake someday and rent a rowboat," Emma said.

"And swim?" Brian asked. "I'm learning how to swim at school camp."

When they finished, Emma suggested they tour the booths the town's merchants set up. There, she bought some scented soap, lotion, some blackberry jam and cookies. Claire found matching tee shirts for the three of them.

They walked to the car. "We've time to stop at the house to leave our spoils and change shirts." She shook her head. "You and Brian have chili on yours."

After the short stop at the house, they drove to Manon's. Brian was excited to find his friend, Jamie, and a girl from his class at the Academy. The three children ran off.

Emma introduced her sister to Rafe, Manon's brother Jay, Maria and Brad Markham. She was surprised to see the doctor here. "Day off, Dr. Markham?"

He nodded and pointed to the children. "That's my Amy with the boys. They're in the same Academy summer class."

Jay grasped their hands. "Good to see you. Maria's with Manon talking about babies."

"Claire and I will join them and leave you men to the grill."

Rafe laughed. "Wait until you see the cake

63

Maria made. Cannolis abound."

"That will be a treat."

She and Claire walked to the women seated beneath a canvas overhang. Emma introduced Claire to Maria. "How have you been?" She studied the dark haired woman and noticed the small belly budge. Emma sighed. Another friend would soon have a baby.

Claire held Rafe Junior. "He's adorable."

Manon smiled. "And growing rapidly. How's our star patient?'

Emma shrugged. "I saw him this morning. I think he's bored."

"Do you know who he is?" Maria asked. "I spent some time with him yesterday."

Emma looked up. "He's an old friend."

"I wonder what he'll do when he's discharged," Maria said.

"Fly to California. I'm sure he can find a doctor there and plenty of women to fawn over him." Emma wanted to bite her tongue. She shouldn't sound so bitter.

"Maybe he'll stay," Claire said.

"Where? He hates any publicity showing him as less than an action figure," Emma said. "Fern Lane Nursing home doesn't restrict visitors."

* * *

Chad finished the second chili dog Rob had had delivered for his dinner. Memories of days at the lake surfaced. He wondered if the area

64

remained divided between town and prep school sides. There had been times when the division had caused fights.

Jeff, his evening guard, gathered the leftovers of the meal. "Fireworks in a couple of hours."

Chad looked at the darkening sky. "You can come in and watch."

"Tempting but this would be a good time for some of those lurkers to attempt trying for pictures."

"Guess you're right." Chad turned on the TV.

Time seemed to crawl but the sky finally grew dark. Fireworks began on the television. He snapped off the set and stared at the night sky. He couldn't stop wishing Emma would change her mind and join him.

The murmur of voices from the anteroom caught his attention. Was this an invasion attempt? He stared at the window and didn't turn to the door. If an invasion, Jeff would send them away.

"I can't do that," Jeff said.

Chad heard the door close. Footsteps clicked on the tile floor. Emma. His heart skipped a beat. The steps paused. He heard a sound he didn't recognize.

Someone touched his arm and massaged. "Surprise."

He pulled his arm away. "What are you doing here?"

Sandra pursed her lips. "I thought we could

make our own fireworks."

Chad sucked in a breath tainted by her cloying perfume. Though she wore a lab coat, the dress beneath shouted seduction. Short skirt, tight bodice and a low scooped neckline revealed she wore no bra.

"Not happening," he said.

She ran her tongue over her fleshy red lips. "I don't see why not. You're known as a man who enjoys women." She leaned toward him. "You've been a week without one." She ran her hands over his chest and downward.

Before she reached her destination, he grasped her wrists. "Don't go there. I'm not interested." Her predatory smile caused him to tighten his grip.

"I could find ways to raise your interest," she drawled.

Chad sucked in a breath to calm anger simmering to a rolling boil. "I don't want to be rude but I will. I'm not interested in you. You're not my type. I choose the women in my life. I've been tempted by women who make you look like an amateur, and I suggest you leave. I want to watch the fireworks in peace."

He released her wrists with a little push. She straightened. "You don't know what you're missing." She left and slammed the door behind her.

That was fun…not. The fireworks began and he lost himself in the bursts of color filling the dark sky. When the display ended, Jeff entered.

"You all right?"

"Yes."

"Glad you sent the lady away. She tried to persuade me to leave my post so she and you could be alone."

"Glad you stayed. I might have needed a rescue."

"You would have. Caught a couple of guys with cameras lurking in the hall. I believe she had a plan."

"Thanks."

The guard grinned. "I'll miss this job when you leave. Brings back my days as a medic."

"Why didn't you go for more medical education?"

Jeff shrugged. "Thoughts of school turned me off. I'm doing extra training on the computer but that's fun." He straightened Chad's bed. "When are you leaving?"

"I have no idea. Depends on how fast I heal. See you tomorrow evening."

The next morning, just after his bed bath and breakfast, his phone chimed. Thinking Rob had news about a place for him to stay when he left the hospital, he answered.

"Chad, where are you?"

Chad roiled his eyes. "I'm fine."

"There are rumors you're a paraplegic or that one or both of your legs have been amputated."

"Gregson, I'll be out of action for the rest of the summer. Both legs were broken. One is in a cast. The other needed surgery and I have to wait for the wound to heal before they put it in a cast, too. I'm in the hospital and not seeing anyone but a few old friends."

"What friends?"

"Did you forget I grew up here?"

"Then the rumors are true. You're in Fern Lake."

"I am."

"I saw pictures of your Ferrari. Are you sure there aren't other injuries?"

Chad laughed. "Other than my legs, I'm great."

Gregson groaned. "It's July. Surely by September you'll be back to work."

"Maybe. Tell the studio my future plans depend on how well I heal. I may need to use a cane. The doctor is concerned about my action life."

"How do you know this doctor knows his business? I can pull some strings and have you seen by the best in the world."

"Goodbye, Gregson. I'll call you when I know what I'm doing."

"Don't hang up. I'm coming to Fern Lake. I'll make nice with the studio and have new contracts when I arrive."

Chad slumped against the pillows. He prayed he would escape before his agent arrived. At least the man couldn't get into his room here without his okay.

That evening Simon arrived before Rob. He sat on the chair beside the bed. "I looked into Fern Lake Nursing and Rehab facility. The place won't work. There are no private rooms and they also refuse to curtail visitors."

Rob stuck his head inside. "No need to look elsewhere. He's coming to my house. I've ordered a hospital bed and a motorized wheelchair to be delivered when I know you're leaving. All we'll need is someone to come mornings and evenings to help you."

Simon nodded. "I have the perfect man." He turned to Chad. "We've planned to start Jeff on learning computer surveillance so he'll be tied up during the day. He can come in the morning and get you settled and then come back in the evening."

Chad nodded. "I like the idea. Now all I need is for the wound to heal and an escape plan."

"We'll devise one," Simon said.

* * *

Time dragged like a slug creeping across the lawn. Chad read the galley for Rob's second book and the idea excited him. He asked Rob to keep him in mind for the movie rights. He spent time writing things he needed to discover for setting up a company to make Rob's book into a movie. He wished he had his computer with all the notes he had from the courses he'd taken. Though he had enough money to finance the first, he didn't want to put everything on one chance. He needed other investors.

Emma hadn't done more than pop in on

rounds and dash away. Days had passed since he'd told her they needed to talk.

His hands fisted. He had to tell her how he felt. The short visits had raised his desire to hold her close. He wanted to convince her he wanted no one but her. He'd been a fool, a child eating flattery and excitement. The time had come to put his life in order and set his plans.

On the morning of the eleventh day of his stay, Dr. Markham arrived. "Time to remove the pins and stitches. A partial cast will be applied for a day. Then a full one. You can leave after that. Any idea where you're going?"

"To Rob Grantlan's and stay until the casts are off."

"Good."

That afternoon after the partial cast was in place, the physical therapist arrived. So did an interesting machine and a wheelchair.

"Grab the bar and lift your tush," the therapist said.

Chad followed the instructions. A pad was slid beneath him. "What now?" he asked.

"We'll use the Hoyer lift to move you into the wheelchair."

A nurse arrived to manipulate the lift while the PT supported his legs. Before long, Chad sat in the wheelchair. The therapist lowered the right leg so the cast rested on the foot rest.

He laughed. "This is great. I may not want to return to bed." He moved to the window. "Looks like the vultures remain."

The PT nodded. "Makes coming to work

interesting."

"I imagine so."

At six, Rob arrived with food. Chad opened the plastic container and tasted the spicy shrimp served over saffron rice. "This is great. Is there a new restaurant in town?"

"It's Rob's Kitchen."

"You're kidding."

"Not a bit. When a man lives alone, he learns to cook unless he wants to eat out every night or call in fast food."

"I see." He didn't but if Rob happily produced gourmet meals, good for him. He would enjoy the results of Rob's culinary skills. "I'll leave here on Monday." He groaned. "I'm not ready to face the world."

"You won't have to. Your room is set up at the cabin. Simon will bring your wheelchair here tomorrow. One of his men will take your place in the hospital's chair while we smuggle you out via the delivery bay."

"Sounds wonderful. What about a paparazzi invasion at your place?"

"Remember the gate?"

"Too vividly." Chad swallowed a mouthful of the spicy dish. "I like the ploy."

Simon strode into the room. He turned to Rob. "Have you told him about the escape plan?"

"Just did. Monday is the day."

"The motorized chair arrives tomorrow."

From the anteroom, Chad heard Janice's voice. He cringed. Rob laughed. "Has she tried to snare you, too?"

"She did. I told her to get lost." He waited to see if she would invade. She didn't. "She was trying to set me up so a photographer could catch us in a compromising position.

"Glad you escaped." Rob leaned back. "You said you planned to do our movie."

"I do. We'll discuss that when I'm at your house."

* * *

Though she'd avoided Chad for days, she heard from the nurses that he was ready for discharge today. Her rounds this morning had taken her to the unit where he was a patient. She completed her notes and paused outside his room. As she entered the anteroom, she saw him seated in a motorized wheelchair.

He looked up. His smile was the one that sent her heart into overdrive. Why did his presence always make her wish for something she couldn't have? He would never change his lifestyle. She hated the thought of becoming close and losing him again.

"Good to see you. Today's the great escape."

"Are you ready to face the crowd?"

He ran his fingers through his dark hair. "Won't happen."

"Why not?"

"There's a plan."

"Where are you going?"

"To Rob's."

She looked toward the window. "Why there?"

"It's a safe place. No paparazzi with cameras. No mikes being thrust in my face. His home is on one level. My evening guard will come mornings and evenings to help me. Rob and I have plans to make."

She didn't want to ask about those plans. She wanted him to return to Hollywood so she could have the final end to her impossible dream.

"How will you escape the crowd outside?"

He explained the plan. His grin reminded her of a boy planning a prank.

Emma shook her head. "Glad you're having fun. Wouldn't an interview or two give them enough to leave you alone?"

He laughed. "They're like sponges soaking up every drop and waiting for more to fall."

"Aren't you responsible for your reputation?"

"Along with my agent." He growled. "I'm tired of being a magnet for attention. I'm tired of being Storm, hero impossible."

"Hope you can change." She turned to leave.

"Hold on a moment." He moved the chair and nearly knocked her down. She grasped the arms of the chair to steady herself. "We need to talk. I'll be at Rob's for a month. Will you come to see me there?" He placed his hands over hers. "You need to know what happened and how much regret I have."

"I don't know."

"I'll give you the combination to the gate."

She straightened. "I'll think about it. I need to go. Office hours start in fifteen minutes." She slipped him a card. "You can reach me here."

Chapter 5

When Emma reached the office, Claire handed her the list of the day's patients. "Did you see Chad?"

"Had patients on the unit where he is so I stopped by. He's leaving today."

"Shame. Did the two of you have that talk?"

Emma shook her head. For some reason she'd avoided the big tell and tell off day. "I didn't have the time. I didn't want to be late for hours."

"When are you planning to tell him? Using an email? He would probably never read the note."

"He's going to Rob Grantlan's cabin until the casts are off. He asked me to visit."

"Go for it."

Emma scowled. Why should she? "I told him to call. He has the office number."

"Why didn't you give him your cell number? What if he tries to call in the evening?"

The look on her sister's face made Emma want to laugh. "The answering service will forward the call."

"Why be so coy?" Claire tapped her pen on

the desk. "Before you can move forward, you must put the past to rest."

Dr. Reid ambled in. "Busy day ahead?"

Claire handed him the list of patients scheduled for the day. "We're booked solid."

He scanned the list. "Not too bad though. What has you both looking so serious?"

Claire leaned forward. "Emma's old boyfriend is in town. He wants to see her. I think she should."

The older man studied Emma. "I would guess he's the reason you're still single."

"Could be." Emma's hands curled into fists. Chad Morgan's hold on her emotions had sent her hurtling into the past.

Dr. Reid touched her hand. "Take your sister's advice. See him and be free."

Emma shook her head. "Enough advice from both of you." She hurried to her office for her lab coat. She didn't know what she wanted to do. Talking to Chad about why he'd stopped calling and texting could show her how foolish hope had been. Maybe his words years ago had been designed to coax her into having sex. Hadn't worked. They had agreed to wait. She had believed he loved her. Though their petting sessions had enticed, she had remained untouched. Did he just want her now because she was the one who had resisted?

She left the office and entered the treatment room to see the first patient on her list.

When her hours ended after going home to shower and change, she drove to Manon'sto deliver more unwrapped presents and to talk about several of the patients. After admiring the baby while Manon opened the bags, Emma settled on a chair across from her friend.

"I think Mr. Bagrin needs a surgical consult. His tests point to some internal problems."

"I agree." Manon looked up. "Has Chad left the hospital?"

"This morning. There was an elaborate escape plan devised to avoid the mob outside."

"So he's back to Hollywood and his platoon of women. You're left hanging again. I'm sure you didn't talk to him."

"You're right there but no Hollywood yet. He'll be at Rob Grantlan's until the casts are off. Guess he didn't want people to see him as a cripple."

"Wasn't seeing Rob his reason for coming to Fern Lake?"

"Yes." Emma scowled. Why else would he be here? Certainly not to see her. Years ago he had walked away leaving her behind. She rose and stood beside the cradle. "When Rafe returned, how did you feel?"

"Happy. Angry. Then fury when I learned what had happened to him. I think you should talk to Chad." She held up her hands. "You must. I avoided Rob for days because I was afraid of what he would say."

Emma released a sigh. "He wants me to come to Rob's. I'm wavering. I'm so afraid I'll cling to an impossible dream."

"You won't know until you talk to him."

Her friend was right but could she accept the truth?

* * *

Chad waited for Rob, Simon and the stand-in to arrive. He was getting out of here. He grinned when he thought about the farce about to unfold. A nurse entered and handed him a sheet of paper. "These are your discharge instructions." She carefully went over cast care and the possible complications. "Don't hesitate to call Dr. Markham if there's any extraordinary swelling or pain."

"Can I shower?"

Her forehead wrinkled. "You could but not in this wheelchair. Also, the cast needs to be kept dry. You have no idea how awful the matting smells when it's wet. Also wet makes a great growing place for mold and bacteria."

Chad groaned. "I'm tired of being part of the great unwashed."

"Haven't the care assistants done complete bed baths?"

"They do but being in the shower and feeling the jets hit my body would feel great."

"Put that on your future pleasure list." She waved and left the room.

Just before noon, Rob, Simon and a man whose body image was close to his arrived. If you didn't study his face and hair he might be thought to be Chad for a short time. The look-alike wore a green tee shirt nearly the same color as the one he wore. The bill of the ball cap cast his face in shadows and the dark shades added to the blurring of his image.

"I wish I could see the reactions of the crowd," Chad said.

Simon laughed. "You will. We'll have a man making a video of the event." He pulled leg casts from a large bag. "Movie props. Took two days to make them."

The nurse arrived and pushed her fake patient into the hall. The day guard followed. Rob lifted the case of Chad's things. Simon opened the door. They headed to the service elevator and rode to the ground floor, moving pass boxes of supplies. At the end, they reached a ramp where a delivery van waited.

Chad wheeled the chair to the ground and up a second ramp into the van. Rob followed and secured the chair to keep it in place. Simon gunned the engine and they wren off.

"Hope all goes well," Chad said.

Rob sat beside the wheelchair. "Have no fear. The local cops are there for crowd control." He opened a tablet and showed Chad the screen. The front of the hospital appeared. "Let's watch the scene unfold."

Chad chuckled. A van from the nursing home parked in the circle. A nurse wheeled the chair with his doppelganger toward the vehicle. Flashbulbs went off. At the top of the ramp into the van, the duplicate pulled off his cap and glasses.

"Move out," Rob said. "I'd like to be home before some smart aleck figures where you've gone."

Twenty minutes later, they reached the gates and the scene of Chad's accident. Simon pushed the sequence of numbers and the gate slid outward. "Welcome to my refuge," Rob said.

Chad's phone chimed. He hit to see who called, hoping to see Emma's name. Then he remembered she didn't know his number. He saw the name and hit answer. "Gregson, what do you want?"

"How did you escape? When I stopped at the front desk, they said you'd been discharged. I witnessed the farce. We need to talk. I have news about the September shoot."

"I won't be ready for action by then."

"They've altered the script."

"We'll talk later. I can't be bothered now."

"Where are you?"

"At a friend's."

"Give me the directions. I'll come with the altered script and the contracts."

"Can't do that. This is a private estate. My friend frowns on visitors. I'll call when I can." He clicked off.

The rear door of the van opened. Rob and Simon clicked a ramp in place and unlocked the chains. They waited for Chad to reach the ground and then replaced the ramp.

Simon saluted. "Good luck. I'll return the van and see you soon."

The door of the house opened. A toddler ran out and grabbed Rob's legs. "You come home."

"I did."

"I go next time."

"We'll see." Rob turned to Chad. "This is Tammy. She's a chatterbox."

Chad smiled. "Hello, Tammy.'

Envy swirled in his thoughts. His life had been full of nothing. He followed the pair into the house. When Andi appeared and kissed Rob, his envy grew. Rob and Andi had rediscovered what they'd shared years ago. Was the same possible for Emma and him?

Andi stepped away from Rob and stood beside Chad's wheelchair. "Hello and welcome. It's great to see you again. Follow me and I'll show you your room."

"Thanks for having me. I'll try not to be any trouble."

"No way to be trouble here." She led the way from the main room into a hall.

Chad sent the chair after her down the wide hall. She paused at the last door and then stepped into a huge bedroom. He saw the hospital bed and the Hoyer lift. Blue sheer curtains covered the wide window. A dark blue bedspread covered the bed. He wheeled to the window and looked down at a large swimming pool.

"I think you'll be comfortable here," Andi said.

"This is great."

She opened a door. "Shower here. Bathroom doorway is large enough for the wheelchair or the lift."

He looked at the shower. "Sure wish I could use that."

She patted his shoulder. "When Jeff comes tomorrow morning, we'll wrap your casts with plastic wrap and plastic bags and hoist you into a shower chair."

"Sounds like heaven," Chad said. "At the hospital there were bed baths but they never seemed enough."

Hs thoughts drifted. What if he'd gone home? There would have been several women fussing over him for the chance of photo ops. That thought left him cold. There was only one woman he wanted fussing over him and he had to find a way to get her to talk to him.

"Chad, hurry," Rob said. "You've made the local news.'

He sped down the hall into the main room in time to see the faked guard reveal herself. "Where is Chad Morgan?" the newscaster asked. "He's been discharged today but no one knows where he has gone."

He and Rob laughed. "They showed the entire video Simon's man took."

"The one I saw a bit of."

"Yes."

Chad studied his friend. His niece sat on his lap. She looked up. "Hungry."

Rob lifted her and stood. "Light lunch today. Soup and grilled cheese."

After they ate, Andi carried Tammy away. Rob cleaned the kitchen. "Have fun this afternoon. It's to work for me."

Andi returned from putting Tammy down for a nap. "Work for me, too. Janine should be here in ten or fifteen minutes to see to Tammy."

Chad remained in the house until the nanny arrived. He left and rode his wheelchair along the path to the swimming pool. He wished he could dive in but even if the casts weren't that heavy, he figured he would sink.

When he returned to the house, he found the tablet Rob had loaned him. After attaching the keyboard, he typed in his plan for the movie company he wanted to begin.

The next day was a repeat of the last. When Rob emerged from his second office stint, he handed Chad a beer. "You okay?"

Chad shrugged. "Yes and no. I envy you and Andi. I wish…"

"Emma?"

"Yah. I blew my chances with her years ago. I can't see a way to make her listen while I kill a crow and cook it."

Rob chuckled. "Don't charge in like a storm trooper. You need to be ready for a marathon. I've been there. Invite her to dinner. I'm cooking."

Chad frowned. "The only number I have is for her office."

"So call. She probably has hours until five. If you reach the answering service, tell them it's an emergency."

83

Chad found his smart phone and the card she'd given him. Before making the call, he returned to his bedroom. If he had to beg, he didn't want his friend to know. He punched the numbers.

"Medical offices of Marshall and Grassi. How can I help you?"

"I'd like to speak to Emma, please."

"I'll check to see if she's available. Who's calling?"

"An old friend."

The woman laughed. "I'm putting you on hold."

Some piece of classical music played. The haunting tune intrigued him. He'd never heard it before. Then he heard a voice. "Hello."

"Emma, it's Chad."

"I saw the clip of your escape. Guess you had help. How did you manage?"

"Down the freight elevator to the loading dock and into a van."

"I'm glad you managed. Bye."

"Don't hang up. Rob and Andi want you to come to dinner tonight."

* * *

Emma gripped the phone. Chad's invitation didn't surprise her but the excitement bubbling through her veins did. She wanted to go. Was that a wise decision? *Remember the promises he'd once made. Remember how he abruptly cut off all communication between us. Remember*

84

all the nights you cried and the days spent cutting memories of him from your thoughts. They could never regain what they had. Did she really want to try?

"Emma, are you there?"

"Yes."

"Will you come?"

She needed to clear the past. "When?"

"Tonight."

Would there be enough time from this moment until this evening to stiffen her spine? His husky voice raised a hope she knew was false. "I don't…"

"Emma, please." He interrupted her refusal. "Don't say no. We really need to talk about the past and why I dropped an important person in my life. I promise we'll talk. We need to put the past to rest."

She released a sigh. Was this the way to go? If he spoke of why he dropped her and she told him of her hurt would she lose the feelings she'd clung to for years? Those things rushed in. She wasn't pretty enough. She had no sense of adventure. She hated the thoughts of leaving her home.

"Emma."

"I'll come. What time?"

"Around six. Press these numbers in the box beside the gate when you get to it and it'll open. Six, seventeen, three, nine. The gate will close automatically. Follow the road to the cabin. Not my idea of a cabin but that's what Rob calls the place. To me the name is an oxymoron. I'll see you then."

Emma disconnected. She slumped against the back of her chair. Had she made the right choice? What would she do if he kissed her again? She felt like a piece of clay waiting to be shaped by a potter. She looked up and saw Claire.

"Patients are waiting."

"I know. Be there in a few minutes."

"What did the hunk want?"

"He invited me to dinner at Rob Grantlan's house this evening."

Claire grinned. "Are you going?"

Emma nodded. "I'm having second thoughts, though."

"Why? You need to let loose all the hurt, disappointment and anger you hold inside."

"I know but you know how I am when I get angry. I cry and feel like a fool."

"Go. Have dinner. The Grantlans will be there. You won't need to be alone with him unless you choose."

She wished Claire was right. Knowing Chad, he would find a way to get her alone. She met her sister's gaze. "I'll go and I will talk."

"Good. You've bottled your anger for too long. I felt so much better after I told Kevin how much he'd hurt me. I also cried."

"How did he react?"

"He hit me and knocked Brian against the wall. I don't think that's Chad's way."

"I don't know him anymore. Who knows what he'll do?" Emma grabbed her stethoscope.

"I'm off to see patients."

For the rest of the afternoon, Emma saw patients and consulted with Dr. Reid. As she finished her records, she tried not to think about Chad and this evening. Claire stopped at the door.

"You almost finished?"

"Another twenty minutes."

"I'm heading to the Academy for Brian."

"See you at home." Her phone chirped. She answered. "Hello, Manon."

"Come for dinner. Rafe has to meet with the evening supervisor."

"Can't. I have plans."

"With?"

"Rob and Andi Grantlan and Chad."

"Have a great time." Manon laughed. "Hit him where it hurts. In his ego."

"I will." Though her stomach churned, she had to talk to Chad and end this whatever-it-was for good.

Emma finished her notes and drove home. Claire and Brian sat in the kitchen. Emma inhaled the aroma of fried chicken. "Maybe I'll stay here for dinner."

Claire shook her head. "I made just enough for us. Don't chicken out."

"I won't." She dashed upstairs and opened her closet to rummage through her clothes. What to wear? She decided against jeans or shorts. She looked at the few summer dresses she owned. Most were too dressy. She pulled a light blue sleeveless dress she'd forgotten she owned. After a quick shower she dressed, brushed her hair and applied lipstick. She slipped on sandals and went downstairs.

"You look pretty," Brian said.

Emma laughed. "Thank you, kind sir."

He giggled. "Not a sir. I'm a boy."

"So you are. See you tomorrow. You be good for your mom."

She left the house and walked to her car. Janice Stone strode up the sidewalk. Emma's shoulders tensed. What did the woman want? She opened the car door.

"Not so fast," Janice said.

"Why are you here?" Emma asked.

"You're Chad Morgan's school friend. I bet you know where he is. I want to see him."

"Why?"

Janice's smile changed to a sneer. "What do you think I want? More time to show him what I can offer him. I'm hotter than those Hollywood women."

"And older," Emma said. "You had your chance. He didn't accept."

"Those guards that were hired made life difficult for me."

"Chad hired the guards. I also heard you arranged a photographer or two to step in and take pictures."

Janice's laughter held a bitter note. "Why shouldn't I? Would have been a way to escape Fern Lake."

Emma opened the car door. "With your degree and experience you could leave any time."

"Not the way I want to resign." She stepped closer. "You're all dressed up. Going somewhere?"

"Yes and I must be on my way."

Janice grasped her arm. "Is it with him? You sure won't give him what he wants, but I will. He's been without a woman for weeks. Tell him to call."

Emma jerked away. She slid into the car and locked the door. For a moment she considered starting the car and removing Janice by force. Her teeth clenched. Why did the woman's desires bother her? Chad could see her or not. The choice was his. She had no intention of forwarding the message.

She knew why. Janice's brashness brought a surge of envy. She felt sure the other woman wouldn't hesitate to show her anger if a man had dropped her. She gripped the wheel. Trusting Chad would be foolish. He thrived on short affairs. She wanted forever. She released an explosive sigh and started the car.

As she drove, a resolve formed. She would tell Chad what his actions and attitude had done to her, how much he'd hurt her. The feeling of not being pretty enough or good enough had been born that day four years ago when she'd called and learned his phone number had been changed. Claire was right. She had to release the anger. How? She couldn't start a fight in front of the Grantlans.

She drove out of town until she reached the

road leading to Rob's home. A car parked on the grassy berm caught her attention. Someone wanting to invade? She stopped beside the box and punched in the numbers Rob had given her. The gate swung outward. A man left the parked car and ran toward the gate. She sped through as the gates closed. Her rear bumper cleared seconds before the gate slid into place. She stopped the car.

The man clung to the gate. "Let me in. I need to speak to Chad Morgan."

Emma eased her car up the hill. The road wound around clusters of trees. When she reached the circular driveway she studied the cabin. She laughed. The front was made from logs but a huge stone wing had been added. Now she knew why Chad had called the cabin an oxymoron. For a moment, she calmed her roiling thoughts. She drew a deep breath and walked to the door.

Chapter 6

Chad wheeled his chair to the front window and peered at the road. He heard the grandfather clock chime quarter past the hour. Would she come? He'd said around six. He'd hoped she'd be early so they would have a chance to talk. Maybe she had changed her mind. She could call but she didn't have his number.

Andi paused behind his chair. "She'll be here. Ask Rob how many times I've been late because an emergency patient needs to be seen or test results must be tracked down."

Chad turned his head. "When we were teens, she always arrived early."

"She has more responsibilities now. I imagine she's changed. People do."

Tammy toddled over. She touched Chad's arm. "I ride."

He laughed. "Climb aboard."

She settled on his lap and touched his cast. "Why you not walk?"

"I broke my legs." He turned the chair and rolled down the hall in the bedroom wing to the end so Tammy could see the pool.

"I swim today. You swim?"

"Can't."

"Even with the bags?"

Chad chuckled. This morning she'd escaped Rob and had run into the bedroom while his casts were being encased in trash bags. Her question amused him. "Not even with the bags. I would sink like the stones you dropped in the pool."

She shook her head. "Okay. You not a fish."

"I sure am not."

He turned the chair and returned to his post at the front window. As he glanced toward the road, a bright blue car appeared over the rise. His heart thundered. His hands felt sweaty. The teenage reaction startled him and made him laugh. Maybe you could go back in time. He might be luckier now than he had been then.

"Lady come." Tammy slid from his lap and ran to the door.

When the bell rang, Andi answered. "Emma, I'm glad you could come." She said something he couldn't hear. Both women laughed.

Emma turned to him. Her laughter made her eyes sparkle. "Thanks for inviting me." She walked to the wheelchair and clasped his extended hand. "How does it feel to have escaped confinement? Claire and I saw the fake you and chuckled at the crowd's reaction."

"So did I. Made quite a show. As to how I feel, half grand. But at least I can go places."

"When I entered the grounds, I saw a car parked on the berm. A man got out and tried to enter the gate before it closed."

"Did he have a camera?"

"I think he carried a briefcase."

His forehead creased. "Was he thin and dark-haired?"

"He was."

Chad groaned. "My agent. He has contracts I'm not ready to sign. He just won't give up trying."

"Why don't you talk to him?" Emma asked.

"I'd have to give him the combination to the gate. There's a good chance he'd arrive with a photographer and a reporter. I'm not ready for that."

Emma cocked her head. "Surely there's a way to open the gate from here."

"I've no idea. Besides, letting him and an entourage in wouldn't be fair to Rob and Andi."

Rob turned from the stove. "I'd just sic chatterbox on him." He tossed pasta into a pan. "Button, go wash your hands. Dinner in ten."

Andi left the room with the toddler. Emma followed Chad to the table. "Smells good."

"Shrimp Diablo." He carried salad, rice and the main dish to the table.

Chad filled glasses with iced tea. When Andi and Tammy returned, the little girl climbed into her highchair. "Eat now."

From a separate dish, Andi fixed a plate for the little girl. "A little less spice than ours. We're educating her palate gradually." She turned to Chad and Emma. "Wine?"

Chad shook his head. "Tea is fine."

Andi filled three glasses. "I forgot you don't like wine."

"I'd have a beer or a rum and cola but not with this food." He lifted his glass of iced tea. "Here's to old friends."

Before long, they ate the delicious spicy meal. Talk covered a dozen topics from politics to art. Stories of the past crept into the conversation. When they finished, the four adults cleared the table.

Rob plucked Tammy from the highchair. "We're going for a walk."

"Find birds and bunnies?" Tammy asked.

"You never know."

Chad reached for Emma's hand. "Would you like to walk, too? There are some nice trails and most I can manage with the wheelchair."

She nodded. "Exercise after all I ate is a good idea."

Chad laughed. "When these casts are gone I'll need to exercise eight hours a day to take off the extra pounds I'll gain. He cooks like this for every meal."

Emma joined his laughter. "How much longer will you have the casts?"

"I've an appointment with Dr. Markham in four weeks. I'll need an X-ray before then." He made a face. "That means a trip to the hospital. With luck the vultures will be after another story and I'll avoid the cameras."

"What will you do without the casts?"

He opened the door so she could follow him. "Exercise in the pool here. I'll need to return to California for several reasons." He steered the wheelchair onto the path leading to the swimming pool. "After my obligations are fulfilled there, I have a great idea for what will come next. I'll be using a cane and have a limp so another Storm adventure is out."

"Does that bother you?"

He shook his head. "I'm tired of that role. I wasn't going to do another Storm even before the accident." He hesitated. "I have a plan but I can't do it alone. I'm working on a way to make a new venture viable."

"Then good luck for whatever."

"Have you ever dreamed of something you would do if you had a chance?"

"Always."

When she said nothing more, he didn't know what more he could say. They continued past the pool and entered the cool shaded area where a bench sat beneath a tall oak. He clasped Emma's hand and tugged her closer. His lips brushed hers. Her hands rested on his shoulders.

Memories of other times they had kissed flooded his thoughts. He eased her down until she sat on his lap. Surely she could feel the effect she had on him.

His tongue darted into her mouth and caught the spices from their dinner. He ran his hand across her chest and felt her breasts. The tips tightened. He wished they had stayed at the house so they could lie on the bed. He cupped one breast and plucked the nipple.

She responded and circled his neck with her

arms. He slid his hand over her belly and found the hem of her dress. His body throbbed with need. The kiss heated. He slid his hand along her thigh and stroked, hoping for her to surrender.

Emma broke free. She stood and glared. "You're good at that but I'm leaving. We came here to talk, not make love." She turned away.

"Stay," Chad said. "We do need to talk. Why are you so upset about a simple kiss?"

She turned. He saw tears in her eyes. What had he done?

"You don't understand."

"Then tell me why responding to my kiss and why wanting me bothers you."

* * *

Emma sank on the bench. The burn of forming tears stirred fury. Why did she always turn into a weeping willow when she tried to express her anger? She clenched her hands. How to begin? The anger bubbling inside moved closer toward release. The thought of the other couple seeing her face after a flood of tears made her want to run and avoid letting loose the pain she'd carried since Chad had stopped calling, texting or sending little gifts.

Not all her anger was toward him. At least half focused on herself and her voluntary responsibilities to see her younger siblings become adults. She could have accepted one of his invitations to visit. He could have come to

Fern Lake. She dragged a breath of air into her lungs.

"Tell me," Chad said. "I never realized how much I missed you until I decided to come to Fern Lake to see Rob. How did we grow so distant?"

She looked up. "I missed you every day. When you first left we emailed. We talked on the phone. We sent each other silly gifts. We shared the good times and the bad ones. I saw your mother several times a week. I made plans to visit you."

"Why didn't you?"

She studied her hands. "For most of those years I had responsibilities. The younger ones needed me."

"Your father was there. And Claire is only two years younger. She could have been there for them."

She glared. "I promised my mother before she died I would see my brothers and sisters grown. I couldn't fail her. Promises must be kept." She stared at him. Did she see a hint of shame in his eyes.

He edged the chair closer. "I'm sure there was more to your holding yourself back. Maybe you were afraid you didn't care."

She drew a deep breath and felt the first tears form. "You talked about how much fun you were having and all the important people you met. Then you had those roles in a half dozen movies. One day, I saw your picture everywhere. Saw you kissing beautiful women.

Read about your latest romance, one after another." Her voice grew shrill. Her cheeks were wet. "You stopped calling. You never texted or emailed me. You were too busy having fun. That's when I knew."

"Knew what?"

"That all the things you told me when we were together were lies."

"No, Emma, they weren't. I love you. I always will. I want to spend the rest of my life with you."

She choked back a sigh and wiped the rapidly flowing tears with her arm. "You only said those things because you wanted sex with me."

Chad shook his head. "That's not true. We both agreed to wait for marriage."

A scream formed. "That didn't stop you from screwing every woman you dated."

"Are you sure that's what I did?"

"I read the stories! Every week a new flavor."

"A lot of that was just promo."

Right." She gasped a breath. "When you found fame. When you saw how all those women wanted you, you cut communication. You were Hollywood's stud. You didn't have the courage to tell me you didn't want me. For months my emails went unanswered. You ignored my texts. Even your mother stopped talking to me. Still I waited just like a fool."

"But...but...Why didn't you call?"

"How could I? Your number changed. You

didn't let me know your new one."

"Gregson," Chad said. "My agent had me take a new number. An unlisted one under Ian Greve. And I never thought to let you know. I'm sorry."

"And I was supposed to know this?" her breath caught in her throat. "You never tried and you certainly looked like you were having fun with your promo ops."

He reached for her hand. She rose and moved away. "Listen to me, please. Those pictures and the women weren't my idea. My agent arranged them. Said I needed an image so I would be chosen for the role of Storm. You have no idea what an unknown has to do. Yes, I did things I didn't enjoy but I had a dream."

Emma used her skirt to wipe her face. "It doesn't matter. I'm leaving. I wish you luck."

"Don't run off. Think of our kisses. They showed you weren't indifferent to me."

Emma drew a shuddering breath. "That's true and that's the problem. For ten years something inside me kept hoping, even during the four years when I didn't hear from you. I'm done with that. I've dated but I couldn't get past my feelings. That's finished. I need to move on the way you have."

Her tears began again. She started toward the path.

"Emma, please," Chad called.

"There's nothing you can do. Go back to Hollywood. Go back to all those blondes who slathered over you."

"I know you care. I've felt how you react to me."

She whirled. "You may be right but that doesn't matter. I'm not waiting another ten years. Thank Rob and Andi for dinner. Goodbye."

She raced up the path and sought refuge in her car. At least she'd left her purse on the front seat. She shoved the key in the ignition and started the engine. Tears blurred her vision. She drove down the hill and stopped to wipe her eyes. Would the gate open?

She released a sigh when the barrier moved. As she pulled onto the road, she noticed the parked car was gone. What now? She couldn't go home. Claire would want to know what had happened.

* * *

Though Chad tried to push the wheelchair to a faster speed, the way was uphill. Emma had reached her car and driven away just as he entered the circular drive. He felt invisible hands squeeze his heart. What she'd said was the truth. When he left to pursue his desire to become a professional actor, he had asked her to wait. Though he could have asked her to join him, he'd known how serious she was about seeing her younger siblings grown. She took her promises as sacred vows.

For years, he had continued to share the events of his life with her. She knew about his work as a stuntman, the acting courses he'd taken and the small roles he'd had and how he'd met Gregson. That meeting had changed his life. Why had he neglected to call Emma and tell her about the new phone number?

"Cut all ties to the past," Gregson had said. "You're on your way to stardom. You have to embrace the life. Parties where you can be seen. Photo ops to increase your exposure. You want starring roles, I'll show you how to get them, but you have to do as I say."

The agent had been right. So much had changed so fast. Suddenly Chad was in demand for small roles as a fighter. Then the script for Storm arrived and he'd forgotten everything about his past and concentrated on becoming Storm.

He drew a shuddering breath. Before Emma had run, she'd said "Goodbye." She had never said that word to him before. His chest ached and felt as if a heavy weight had landed. He refused to believe he couldn't find a way to let her know how much he cared. Damn the accident and these broken legs that kept him from pursuit. He would find a way. He must.

Andi, Rob and Tammy emerged from the trees. "Where's Emma?" Andi asked.

"She just left. She sends thanks for dinner."

"When's she coming back?" Rob asked.

Chad gripped the arms of the chair. "I don't know."

Rob carried Tammy to the house. Andi lingered. "Are you okay?"

"Not really, but there's nothing you can do. She told me some things I needed to hear. I never realized how badly I'd hurt her several years ago. I can't change what I did and I can't think of a way forward."

"Give her time." Andi patted his shoulder. "She's a very contained person. I can understand how she feels. She needs time."

"Since I'm grounded for a month or so I can give her time." He started the wheelchair. "There has to be away to spend time with her."

Andi grinned. "Use your imagination."

"At the moment mine is dead."

"You'll find a way." She walked to the house. "Time to put Tammy to bed."

"I'll be along later." Chad sat and stared at the darkening sky. He replayed the scene with Emma, trying to find a way to change what had gone down. He couldn't. The moon rose and stars appeared. The sultry night breeze flowed over his skin.

Finally he turned the chair and rode to the door. He pushed and the door flew open and banged against the wall.

Rob stepped from the kitchen. He held a bottle of beer. "You do like making grand entrances. Good thing the wall is sturdy."

"I didn't expect the door to open at a touch. Couldn't reach the knob."

"You could have rung the bell."

"What I did captured your attention." He pointed to the bottle Rob held. "Is that for me?"

Rob chuckled. "Am I corrupting you? You

seldom drink."

"Maybe I've changed."

Rob opened the fridge and took out another. He twisted off the cap and handed the bottle to Chad. "What happened?"

"Nothing." Chad paused. "Too much."

Rob shook his head. "If nothing happened why did she leave?"

"It's complicated."

"Life usually is."

"She doesn't want to see me again. Damn, I was such a jerk. I listened to Gregson when I signed on with his agency. You need to change your image. Be a playboy. Wow the ladies. Show off your physical talents. Everything you do is a photo op. Forget the past." He groaned. "So many of my encounters were nothing more than publicity."

"What did you do to Emma?"

Chad gulped a mouthful of peer and swallowed. "Didn't let her know my new phone number. Stopped letting her know my romances were fakes. I never kept in touch with her after Gregson controlled my career."

Rob raised his bottle. "Sounds like you have a lot to overcome. I know how hard eating crow can be. Give her time." He walked to the couch. "What are you going to do while waiting for your bones to heal?"

Chad wheeled the chair to face his friend. "Several things. One is to figure how much of my assets I can use to make your first book into a movie. Gregson has been no help there. He just drools over the money a new Storm will bring."

"I suppose making a movie is expensive."

"Depends. Some are made with little cash outlay but I don't want this to be an amateur production."

"How many people would you need to hire?"

"A lot. There's lighting, cameras, sets, costumes, makeup people. I'm sure there are dozens more areas. Think of the list of names you see at the end of a movie. This isn't counting the actors and extras."

"What about the director?"

"That's my next goal. I want to produce, direct and star. All three. I'll hire an experienced assistant director."

"Do you have to fund the entire project?" Rob asked. "I've got money just collecting interest and Andi insists she worked too hard to become a practitioner to quit. What about forming a company?"

Chad grinned. "Come into my parlor."

"I'm willing to be caught. Come to my study and we'll start a file."

"Already have one. Let me get the tablet." He handed Rob the beer. "You bring this and maybe some coffee."

Before long they were in Rob's study. He opened his computer and transferred the file from Chad's tablet. "Will we need music?"

"For background. I'm not ready to tackle a musical. Why do you ask?"

"I'm thinking of a third member for the group. You remember Jay Lockley?"

Chad nodded. "A whiz at the piano."

"He's done music for movies. He might be interested in investing. Who else will we need?"

"An attorney."

"I know one. Bate Forbes handles my book contracts and my other affairs. I'll ask him."

"We'll need a studio with space for sets. I thought we might tap Simon and his partner for security and maybe to scout properties."

"Good thought. So you think we won't have to relocate to Hollywood."

"If we can find the space here we can set up shop in Fern Lake. Much of the book takes place in a small city. We'll need some interior shots and one or two scenes at the hospital." He groaned. "I'm stuck here so I can't explore to find a place."

"Not to mention the crowds you would gather."

Chad laughed. "There is that."

"I'll call Simon tomorrow and see what he can do," Rob said.

"I'll call him," Chad said "You need your writing time."

"And you need something to do but I will call the other two and set up a meeting."

Chapter 7

Emma halted her car at the gate and was surprised they opened. She drove through and it closed behind her. The car she'd seen parked wasn't there. She imagined Chad's agent had become tired of sitting in the car and hoping to slip onto the estate.

As she pulled onto the road, she debated where to go. Definitely not home, not yet. Facing her sister's curiosity didn't suit her. Where then? She thought about Manon and shook her head. Rafe would have returned home from his meeting by now.

She had no desire to hit one of the local bars. The diner where she and her friends had once hung out held no interest. As she drove toward town, she reached the road leading to the lake. It was late, here was a place where she could walk and think. In the past she'd come here when acting as a substitute mother had depressed her spirits. A few cars remained in the lot. She parked, left the car and walked down the path to the lake. The bright moon in a cloudless sky provided light.

As she ambled along the edge of the water, her thoughts turned to Chad and the kiss. The same sensation of warmth and arousal flooded her body. She released a sigh. The kiss, his touches and caresses, they'd brought a rush of desire she couldn't deny. Thank heavens she had enough sense to put distance between her and temptation. Much more time and she would have given herself to him.

Tears smarted her eyes. Realization spewed like an erupting volcano. She still loved him. That created a dilemma. She wanted to be free and she wanted to walk away. She couldn't let him know the kiss had ruined her plans to end her longing for a happy forever with him.

How could she have thoughts of a life with him? His lifestyle shouted danger. His affairs with women, though he'd said some were arranged for publicity, would drive her into storms of envy and jealousy. She wanted a man to be hers alone. She refused to become a photo op.

Her thoughts scattered. She turned and retraced her steps. Chad could change. She laughed. Would a man used to women swarming him like bees, each wanting to be his queen ever settle for just one? She didn't know and had no way to learn.

A scream built. She'd had choices. She'd dated a half dozen men but turned them all away. Her chest ached. She reached the car and slumped in the driver's seat. She must push those dreams away and learn to live with a second choice. She started the car and drove home.

When she pulled into the driveway, only the porch light glowed. She let herself in and hurried to her room. She grabbed a sleep shirt and went to shower, hoping to wash away the touches of Chad's kisses and touches. Not possible. She drew on her sleep shirt and walked to bed.

Claire sat in the chair beside the window. Emma swallowed a groan. Soon the questions would begin. She wasn't ready to answer.

"Did you have a good time? It's nearly midnight. I was worried."

"It's only a few minutes after eleven." Emma sat on her bed. "I left at nine and drove around a bit to think about the evening."

"What happened?"

Emma released a held breath. "He kissed me. He apologized for his actions in the past. I don't believe him." She didn't mention Chad's declaration of love.

"Why not?"

"I'm just the flavor of the week."

"Why not give him a chance?"

"Why should I?"

Claire rose. Her hands rested on her hips. "You've been obsessed by him for years. How can you be sure he hasn't changed?"

Emma uncoiled her fisted hands. "You've seen the life he lives. While he was in Hollywood, I could dream he would come to his senses. Then I remembered he's a Leo. Leos thrive on attention. He'll never change. I'm tired of being a fool. Unfortunately, Cancers tend to

108

cling to old things."

"Just take a chance."

"Would you if Kevin…"

Claire scowled. "Kevin broke our marriage vows. He saw other women. He scared me and Brian with his threats. He hit me repeatedly. Unless you and Chad snuck off and married, he was a free agent."

"Go to bed. We have to work tomorrow."

"Night. Just think about what you want." Claire closed the door behind her.

Emma slid beneath the sheet. She had to think but she needed to sleep. Tomorrow would be a busy day. Before long she drifted away.

Troubled dreams. Searching. Following Chad, always reaching but never touching. The kiss replayed again and again.

The sun streaming through the lace curtains woke her. She rolled on her side and turned off the alarm. After a short visit to the bathroom, she dressed in gray slacks and a blue sleeveless blouse and combed her hair. After eating a bowl of cereal and drinking two cups of coffee, she walked to her car. Brian and Claire waved.

At the hospital she made rounds, wrote orders and discussed the results of tests with two patients. This done, she drove to the office.

A call from Dan interrupted her lunch. "I'm in town until tomorrow afternoon. Let's hook up for dinner."

"Where and what time?"

"Seven at Louie's."

"See you there.' Though she and Dan had

never been anything but friends, being with him would give her a break from obsessing over Chad.

* * *

That morning while waiting for Jeff, Chad reviewed the plan he and Rob had begun, He ran a finger down the list and thought of several items to add.

A knock sounded on the door. "Come in."

He nearly laughed. Jeff carried the supplies for the wrapping. "Do you have enough for the job?"

"Andi said one roll of the wrap is nearly gone. Where she found this massive one is beyond me." He dropped the supplies on the bed and walked back to close the door. "So Curious Miss doesn't wander in. One morning of her help was enough."

Chad laughed. "Remember the wad of wrap she tried to stick on my cast."

"Too well." Jeff quickly finished one cast and began on the second.

A half hour later, Chad sat on a shower chair with a second one to prop his casts. From a dozen directions water pulsed his body. He quickly washed and was hoisted from the chair. His casts lay on a metal tray and Jeff eased the lift into the bedroom. Once dried and dressed, he and Jeff moved to the main room.

"I'm off to fight with the computers," Jeff said. "See you this evening."

"Have fun."

"I will."

Rob turned from the stove. "French toast and sausage patties this morning. There's syrup, honey and several kinds of jam."

"I'll weigh a ton before these casts are off," Chad said.

The doorbell rang. Chad wondered if he could hide. Rob placed the platter on the table and walked to the door. "Just a delivery. Jeff let him in as he left. He carried a box. "Your computer. The tablet is great for quick things but you need more space and power. After we eat, I'll set it up. You can transfer your lists and spend time on the internet." He filled mugs with coffee.

Tammy dashed into the room. A young woman ran after her. Tammy ran to Rob. "Up, up."

He scooped her into his arms and put her into the high chair. After they ate, Rob rose. "I'll set up the computer and get to work. Chad, this is Janine, Tammy's nanny. Chad is a friend and broken. He's an anonymous man."

"I understand," Janine said.

"I ride," Tammy said.

"Not this morning. After lunch."

"Okay."

Before long, Chad sat in the bedroom at the desk. He transferred his files to the computer. He couldn't resist reading the latest gossip about his accident and his whereabouts. An interview with Gregson made him shake his head. "He'll be back better that before. Once he finishes rehab, he'll begin filming *Storm 5*."

Chad closed the article. He needed to talk to Gregson but not until he had his plan in order. He reached for the phone to call Simon. "You busy?"

"Not at the moment."

"I have something to ask you."

"Problem with Jeff?"

"Not a bit. I want to talk to you about empty warehouses."

"Why?"

"We need a place to set up for a studio."

Simon laughed. "Then you and Rob are going through with the movie. I'll make some calls and see if I can take you on a tour."

"That'll be a bit difficult, especially if someone recognizes me."

"Right. I'll arrange a virtual tour. I'll call you later."

While Chad waited for the call, his thoughts turned to Emma. There must be a way to show her he was changing his life. Just thinking about her caused him to pulse with anticipation. He'd never felt this way about any woman in his life.

Was there a way to capture her interest? An idea popped into his head. He searched sites on the internet and found one for flowers and fruit. He laughed. He'd found a way.

Before he had a chance to order, Simon called. "Check your computer. Do you have Live Chatter?"

Chad studied the icon display. "I do."

"Log on. It may take a few minutes. You'll need to create a user name and a password."

A short time later, Chad had an account. "I'm in. Do I need to hang up?"

"Unless you want double sound, do. I've found what might be the right place. It's five miles from town. About seven acres of property. Two buildings. One's a warehouse. The other's offices."

"Sounds good. I'm hanging up."

"I'm recording this on video. This might be the right one." He showed the two buildings. "There's a stone wall around the property. Lots of room for parking and for creating sets. You and Rob can watch the video later."

Chad watched as Simon showed interior shots of the long one story building and the smaller three story one. "This is great." Ideas flowed into his head.

"There are two other properties," Simon said. "Do you want to see them?"

"Just make videos of them," Chad said. "You have an eye for what's needed."

Simon chuckled. "How about a share or two in the company?"

"That could be arranged."

"I'll stop by later today."

Chad leaned back. He glanced at the clock. Two hours until Rob's lunch break. Get to work. He returned to the site he'd found and sorted through the selections. He found a whimsical arrangement of cacti for today and an arrangement of fruit tor tomorrow. Choosing anything else stymied him. He doubted she would be at the office on Saturday and Sunday. Where did she live?

He thought of the house where she'd grown up and decided that was too large for one person. Didn't she say Claire and her son lived with her? Maybe Rob knew. He would ask later.

Rob appeared in the doorway. "Ready for lunch?"

"I am. Simon will arrive this evening with views of property we can see." He didn't mention his thoughts on the place he'd liked. Rob had a say.

"Good. Jay and Nate, he's my attorney, will be here this evening and we'll try to bring them into the company."

* * *

Just after lunch, Emma prepared to see her afternoon patients. Claire stepped into Emma's office. She carried a plant. Not an ordinary one but an array of cactus. Three cacti surrounded a rundown shack and a hill with a sign. *Last Chance Mine*. "This is yours why?"

"An old joke about my black thumb." Emma burst into laughter and opened the card. The words turned her laughter into a giggle.

"What's so funny?" Claire asked.

Emma drew a deep breath. "To my prickly friend from a man whose ego you thoroughly pricked. Sorry I was a jerk, Chad."

Claire shook her head. "Wonder where he

found them."

"Who knows?" Emma put the arrangement on the windowsill. The gift reminded her of the silly presents he had sent to her from California years ago.

"What are you going to do about this?" Claire asked.

Emma shook her head. "Not much I can do. I'd like to thank him but I don't have his number. I'm certainly not calling Andi and asking to speak to him." Doing that would make her feel foolish. If Chad wanted to talk to her he would have to call the service. She turned to the door. "Patients are waiting."

* * *

Chad wondered how Emma had liked the cactus display. He also was on edge. After dinner, the men who might be interested in the plan he and Rob had devised would be arriving for a meeting after dinner.

This evening Rob fired the grill and broiled the steaks marinated in beer and herbs all day. He also grilled potatoes and vegetables. Chad glanced at the clock. Soon the men would arrive.

Andi carried the dishes from the table. "I hope you don't mind but tomorrow Rob, Tammy and I will be gone for most of the day. We'll be at the lake. My partners are having a picnic."

"I'll be fine." Chad smiled. The card with

today's gift had contained his phone number. If Emma didn't call, he would call her answering service and plead an emergency.

"Good," Rob said. "There are things in the fridge for sandwiches." A short time later the first of the men arrived. Simon carried a tape. "Do you want to see this now or wait for the others?"

"We wait," Rob said. He pointed to the monitor. "Our other guests are on the way. We'll watch the video here and then head to my study." They settled to eat.

Chad met Jay and Nate. They settled on the couch and watched the video of the three places Simon had visited.

"Number one is the right one," Chad said. "We'll need to rent the property."

"Agreed," Rob said.

"Will you tell me what this is about?" Nate asked.

"Come to my study." Rob lifted a huge thermos. "Coffee. We'll need it. Time to explain our plan."

A different kind of excitement stirred. Chad rode to Rob's office and opened the computer to the plans. He turned to the attorney. "We'll have a lot of business for you. There will be contracts and a partnership agreement." He began to explain about Rob's book and his rights to make the movie.

"Do you mean to direct?" Jay asked.

Chad nodded. "I've been taking all kind of classes. I'm ready to leave the rough and tough roles I've been forced to take."

He and Rob took turns explaining their plans. "We want to locate in Fern Lake," Rob said. "That's the reason for the video."

Jay looked up. "I'm in for the music end but I want to have a share in the company. I'm sure I'm good for the same amount as you put in."

Chad stared. "That takes gut. We could lose all."

Jay grinned. "I've read Rob's book. You say you have a treatment. Make me a copy and I'll tinker with some tunes."

"I'll send it over tomorrow," Rob said.

"We'll make this a limited company," Nate said. "Three major share holders."

"Five on the board. The five of us," Chad said. "First thing is to rent the property." He laughed. "I'll make another list."

Nate took notes. "I'll write this up and get copies to all of you."

Rob poured coffee for all. "There may be other people who want to invest. Do we take them on?"

Chad shook his head. "This is ours. I'll start making lists of equipment we'll need and try to interest some people I know for some of the technical jobs."

"You really need to talk to your agent," Rob said.

"I will. Maybe next week. I need to call Dr. Markham for that letter he promised."

The attorney nodded. "I'd like to see the

property. Might be better to buy than rent."

"We'll go on Monday." Simon said.

Before long they left. Chad returned to his room. Jeff arrived to help him into bed. As he settled to sleep, he thought about Emma. He hoped to hear from her.

* * *

Emma was sitting in her office on Friday afternoon when Claire and Karen walked in. "Another gift," Claire sad. She placed a bouquet of fruit turned into flowers on the desk.

"You are so lucky," Karen said. "Who's your admirer?"

Emma snatched the card before the other two could. She tucked the card in her pocket. "Enjoy. I'm off to see patients."

"What does the card say?" Claire asked.

"Later," Emma said.

Emma engrossed herself in the patients. What was she going to do? She'd figure that out later when she was alone. The moment the others left, she completed her records. Then she popped a strawberry into her mouth and fingered the card. Should she call?

Finally she tapped the number into her cell. A moment later she heard his deep voice. "Hello."

"Chad, no more flowers or fruit to the office, please."

"Didn't you like them?"

She laughed. "Of course I did but Claire's

118

and the office nurse's curiosity is driving me crazy."

"I would have sent them to you at the house but I don't know where you live."

"I live where I always did." She kicked off her heels and rested her feet on the desk.

"Isn't the house too big for one?" he asked.

"When Dad retired and moved to Florida, three of the youngers still lived there. They were in college. I bought the house so they would always have a home."

"So now I know. Shame I can't come to visit. I have great memories of those days. Do you still have the great porch swing?"

"There's a swing but a new one. The one you remember died of old age." She closed her eyes. That's where she had her first kiss, one evening after she and Chad had done homework.

A buzzing sound caught her attention. She dove from dreams of the past. "The office phone. Hold on while I answer." She lifted the receiver. "Yes. I'll be there in ten." She hung up. "Chad, they need me at the hospital. Got to go."

"Duty."

"Afraid so. I'll talk to you tomorrow."

"I'll be around."

"Bye." She rose and left the office. Her smile grew. Almost like the old days.

The next day after rounds, she returned home to complete the housework and to pack for the short trip they planned. The doorbell rang. Brian ran to answer. "Aunt Emma, come quick."

Emma ran to the porch and burst into laughter. The delivery man held a huge plush bear with the same colors as the one Chad had won for her at the fair years ago. She took the creature and read the note. "Shows how much my love has grown."

Claire shook her head. "What next?"

"I don't know. Let me take this up to my room. Then we'll finish cleaning and packing."

"Aren't you going to call him?"

"Later."

When the cleaning spree ended, Emma sat on the swing and hit Chad's number. "The bear arrived and thank you for the memories."

"Where are you?" he asked.

"On the porch swing."

"I hoped you were in your room and we could indulge."

She laughed. "You're moving too fast."

"I know. What do you plan for the rest of your day?"

"Claire and I are taking Brian to Playland. We're staying overnight."

"Oh." She heard disappointment in that one word. "Have a great time. Call me when you have a chance."

"Aunt Emma," Brian called. "We're ready."

"So am I. Chad, I'll call later."

During the two hour ride to the small amusement park, Brian chattered and kept

Emma's thoughts from Chad and what she wanted do about him.

They spent the afternoon and early evening at the park watching Brian on the rides, riding others with him and playing games. Emma won two bears. She gave one to Brian and decided Chad deserved the other. She headed to the room they shared, too tired from the day spent in the sun to call Chad.

On Sunday, they checked out of the motel and went to the park. Brian rode all his favorite rides. Emma bought three boxes of fudge, one for Chad, one for the house and the last for the office. After dinner, they drove home.

Before she unpacked, Emma called Chad. "I'm back."

"Did you have fun?"

"Yes, and I'm exhausted. Too much sun."

"Can you come tomorrow and have dinner here?" he asked.

"I think so. I'll see you then."

After office hours, Emma hurried home to change clothes. She picked up the fudge and the bear and drove to Rob's estate. At the gate she let herself in. When she reached the house, Chad waited outside.

"I've a gift for you," he said.

"Great minds. I've two for you." She handed him the bag with the logo of the park on the bag. She opened hers and found a book of poetry. "John Donne. You remembered."

He nodded. "I remember everything. Your grandfather used to read these poems to you."

"He did." She waited for him to open the bag.

He pulled out the bear and laughed. "I have a feeling the imp will steal this." Then he saw the fudge. "You remembered my sweet tooth." He opened the box and took a piece. He bit and then offered her a bite.

His fingers lingered on her lips. Her tongue flicked out to take the rest of the candy. One hand drew her head closer and their mouths met. A blast of chocolate flavored the kiss.

Reluctantly, she stood. "Didn't you invite me for dinner?"

"I did. Rob's doing chicken on the grill and there are strawberries for dessert."

"Sounds wonderful."

After a delicious dinner, she and Chad walked past the pool just as they had before. He told her of the plans he and Rob had made for forming a movie company.

"We've even found a place for the studio and intend to buy. It's five miles from town. Negotiations are taking place and I'll be in touch with some people to head different areas."

She frowned. "What does this mean?"

"I'm returning to Fern Lake for good."

The joy in his eyes delighted her but a nagging doubt tickled her thoughts. Would he be content not to be the star and in the spotlight? "What if..." She didn't want to think his plans would fail. "Won't you miss the money you earn?"

He laughed. "I've been frugal and invested

smartly. I could never work another day and still manage to live in good style."

"Good for you."

He made a face. "As soon as I can move about I'll need to go to Hollywood for a number of reasons. To sell my house, pack up what I want to bring and settle the contracts for the Storm movies."

"Have you talked to your agent?"

"Not yet. He won't be happy when he reads the letter from Dr. Markham. Good thing I put off signing the contract for the fifth and sixth version of Storm. Enough business. Come here."

Emma moved closer. He pulled her into an embrace. Their mouths met in a fierce kiss. He groaned. "I can't wait until I'm free of these casts. I'd really like to move on from kisses."

She ran her hands over his chest. "We could...Like in the old days." Her fingers slipped beneath the band of his shorts.

He grasped her wrist. "Though that would be wonderful, there's no way to clean me out here. Another time I'll plan better."

For a while they kissed and then returned to the house. Emma popped in to tell Andi and Rob good night.

Chad went to the car with her. "Tomorrow?"

"Evening hours for patient convenience."

"When will your partner return?"

"The middle of August." She kissed him and opened the door. "Enjoy your candy. I l love the book. Night."

"Night. I love you."

As she drove away, she thought about his words of love. She hadn't said them back. Maybe she never would. Some of her doubts remained.

Chapter 8

Andi and Rob returned from the grocery store. Chad met them at the car and accepted a bag of groceries. Plans for making Rob's book into a movie had progressed. Simon and Nate had arrived with the contract for the purchase of the lot. An architect and contractor had been reached and would be arriving to talk about the needed changes in the space.

Andi followed Chad into the house. "You need to do something about that man parked outside the gate. He was nearly hurt trying to get in while the gate closed."

Chad drew a deep breath. "You're right. Can the gate be opened from here? I wouldn't trust Gregson with the combination. The man believes the world runs on promo ops."

Rob nodded. "Just let me know when."

"How about now?" Chad pulled out his phone and keyed in Gregson's number. He waited for an answer.

"It's about time," Gregson snapped. "I've called dozens of time and they go straight to voice mail."

Chad's hands clenched. "I've needed the time to come to grips with my new normal.'

"What are you talking about?"

"I'll tell you when I see you. Rob will open the gate. You have five minutes to drive through. Park in the circle and ring the doorbell. Only you. No photographers or reporters."

"I hear you. I'm alone."

"Drive to the gate." He watched Rob activate the gate. "Send him back to my room. We may be some time." He turned the chair and rode down the hall. He reached his room and located a copy of the letter from Dr. Markham. He opened the computer and pulled up his plan.

As he sat by the window and stared at the pool, he wished he could shed these casts and dive into the water. Wrapping the fool things the way they did for his shower would keep the cast from getting wet but the weight would sink him. He laughed as an image formed in his thoughts.

"Chad."

Gregson's sharp tenor tone snapped his laughter. He turned the chair. "Good morning."

"Is that all you can say?"

"For right now while I'm in a wheelchair."

The slender man sat in the chair near the computer. "I'll admit this is a nice place to rest but you're losing tons of opportunities for publicity. More of the paparazzi have given up and have left town. Others are snagging the ops you're missing."

"I'm glad to hear the vultures are leaving."

Gregson opened his briefcase. "I've had a long talk with the studio powers. They've designed a new opening scene for movie five."

Chad gulped a breath. "You need to read this letter from Dr. Markham."

Gregson scanned the paper then crushed it into a ball. "This is unacceptable. What does he know?"

"He's a skilled surgeon. He's Board certified. Young. He finished his training a year ago and had his residency at a top notch hospital."

"We'll get a second, third and fourth opinion and find someone to say this recommendation is nonsense."

"We will not. This is my body and my career. You'll need to let the studio know now Storm is dead."

"Damn it, no."

Chad shrugged. "I've made my peace with the news."

"What are you going to do?"

Chad smiled. "Rob and I along with three friends are forming a film company. Our first venture will be turning Rob's book into a film."

"But the studio is interested. I told you that before. They even have several stars lined up for the major roles."

"They can't do that. I have the film rights."

"They've talked to your friend's agent. She's angry nothing has come of your plans. She'll talk to Rob. He'll see the need to put an end to your ideas."

Chad laughed. "Not happening. Our plans are taking form. We've signed contracts and our studio will be ready this fall."

Gregson scowled. "So how will the studio handle you leaving Storm?"

"Build his protégée into the star. Start the next film with Storm's death."

"I like it but not sure I can sell the idea." He looked at the crumpled paper he'd tossed on the floor. "I shouldn't have destroyed that."

"You're in luck. That's a copy. I made several." He pulled a clean one from the desk, folded and put it in an envelope. "Here."

Gregson nodded. "You'll still need to come back and talk to them."

Chad scowled. "I will in a month or so. The casts will be on for at least two more weeks. Then I'll need to learn how to walk again."

"I'll see you then and all will be set. I'll call if there's any problem." He sighed. "I still wish you would do the two movies. The money we're losing is massive."

Chad followed his agent and waited until the car drove away. Another problem solved. He couldn't wait to tell Emma. Except he wouldn't see her tonight. She had late office hours. He returned to his room to plan his next step toward winning her.

He'd told her he loved her. She hadn't made the same confession. She enjoyed the kisses. She seemed to want more except she'd easily accepted his reason for not making the petting session more sensual.

In his room, he searched the web. Candy would be his next move. He spent an hour looking at different specialty shops. Then he found one that made raspberry creams. She had always loved them. He ordered a box of both dark and milk chocolate raspberry creams and had the order sent overnight mail so she would have them tomorrow.

For Thursday he found a jeweler in town that sold gold charms so the one he ordered could be delivered on Thursday.

This done, he went out to the main room to visit with his friends.

* * *

On Wednesday when Emma returned from the office, she found a large box had been delivered. She grinned. What had Chad done? When she opened the box, inside she found a box of chocolates. She read the card. He had remembered another of her favorites. Raspberry creams.

She took one of the dark chocolate pieces and bit. A burst of bitter chocolate blended with the sweet flavor of the creamy fruit center. She'd never tasted one so delicious. She offered the box to her sister and Brian. "Just one," she said to her nephew.

Claire tasted hers. "These are wonderful. I suppose you'll be headed to see him this evening."

Emma nodded. "But not until after dinner. Wouldn't want to miss the gravy that's been simmering all day."

Claire laughed. "We've made a lot and I'll

freeze what we don't use. Did you use Dad's recipe? The one he stole from Uncle Louie?"

"Borrowed," Emma spoke the words their father always said.

Once they'd eaten and dishes were done, Emma drove to Rob's estate. Chad met her at the door. "Thought you might come for dinner."

"Couldn't, we made Dad's gravy."

He groaned. "Not fair." He turned to Rob. "She has a recipe for red sauce that rivals Louie's."

Rob sauntered over. He draped an arm around her shoulders. "Can you be bribed?"

She laughed. "With the right offer."

"Just how good is this sauce?" Rob asked.

"As good as Louie's. I told you," Chad said.

Emma giggled. "That's because it's the same. Dad and Louie inherited it from their mother and grandmother. He's my uncle. I'll share the recipe someday but you must swear never to reveal the gravy sauce to anyone who isn't a blood relative."

"For that I'll swear." Rob kissed her cheek. "Time to tuck the imp in for the night."

When he left, Chad pulled Emma close for a kiss. "How was your day?"

"Busy as always. And yours?" She settled next to the wheelchair and held his hand. This kind of sharing was wonderful.

"Been organizing things for the movie. Saw my agent yesterday."

"How did that go?"

"He's returned to Hollywood to speak to the studio. He was upset about Dr. Markham's letter but he'll show it to the studio. Wanted me to get more opinions but I refused."

"So all is well."

He grinned. "Not as I wish. I figure maybe two weeks will see me with my cast gone. I can't wait."

"Then you'll have hard work."

He winked. "No harder than persuading you to trust me again."

"I wish things were different."

"I love you. I'll keep saying that until you believe." He drew her hand to his mouth and kissed her fingers. "I'll keep trying. I'm not going back to the kind of life I lived before."

How much she wanted to believe him. "Time," she said.

* * *

The next morning, Rob carried dishes to the table. Chad helped. He opened the refrigerator and maneuvered his chair so he could reach the pitcher of orange juice, the milk and butter.

Rob turned. "We have a small problem. Been putting it off since you moved in."

"And that is?"

"My mother and Hattie are in Virginia for a visit with friends. They want Andi and me to bring Tammy for a visit. I'm not comfortable with leaving you alone."

"You can. Jeff will be here mornings and

131

evenings. How long would you be gone>"

"We'll leave Friday and return Tuesday. I could go alone with Tammy."

"That's a long trip to take with a child.' Chad straightened. "I have an idea that will fit into my plans."

"What is that?"

"I'll ask Emma if she can at least come on Saturday and Sunday. I'm not at all sure she'd stay over but she could be here for lunch and dinner."

"That could work."

"Maybe Jeff could stay a bit in the morning. I'll speak to him."

Rob laughed. "He could stay over, too."

"Not my first choice." As Rob walked away, Chad began to plan. He went to his room, opened the computer and found the charm he wanted for Emma. He remembered the gold charm bracelet she'd worn. He hadn't; seen her wearing it since his return but it was impractical for work. The jeweler would deliver the charm this afternoon. He told Rob about the delivery and learned how to open the gate for the delivery.

After Rob showed him how, Chad laughed. "This solves lunch and even dinner while you're away. Makes life simpler if Emma has other plans."

"I'll provide you with a list of restaurants that will deliver." Rob finished eating. "I'm off to work. Not much to do today."

Moments later, the nanny arrived and took

charge of Tammy. Chad went outside and rode around. He thought of a way he might entice Emma for part of a day on Saturday. She could bring Claire and Brian and they could use the pool.

That afternoon the charm, a heart, arrived. He couldn't wait for Emma's visit. She finally arrived at seven. They took a walk.

He handed her the jeweler's box. She frowned. "You didn't."

"You're right. Just open it."

When she did, she laughed. "For my bracelet."

He nodded. "It's my heart and I give it to you."

She looked away. "I hope you won't regret doing that."

"Never." He halted and took a breath. "Do you still have the bracelet?"

"Yes, but I seldom wear it. Not good for work."

"There's something I need to ask you."

She looked up and he saw hesitation in her expression. "Rob and Andi are taking Tammy to Virginia to visit his mother. Do you think you could spend the weekend here?"

"I could," she said. "When do they leave?"

"Tomorrow and return on Tuesday."

"I could come Friday after work but I have weekend rounds."

"Jeff will be here morning and evenings. I thought on Saturday you could bring Claire and Brian to use the pool."

"That's nice. Brian would like that. He's learning to swim at school."

"Rob is giving me a list or restaurants who deliver."

"No need. We've a gallon of red gravy in the freezer. Enough for a meal or two."

"If it's no trouble you can provide Saturday and Sunday dinner." He laughed. "Rob will be sorry he won't be here." He turned the chair. "Let's go in and tell them. I'll have Friday's dinner delivered."

* * *

On Friday as Emma left the office she wondered if she'd made the right decision. By spending the weekend with Chad, she had made a commitment. Her emotions darted from looking forward to spending time with him and deciding not to go.

She locked the office door and went to her car. Instead of speeding off she sat with the keys clutched in her hand. Should she go? She knew she must for she'd made a promise. Finally she started the car and drove away from town. She stopped at the gate to let herself in. After she parked, she carried her canvas bag to the house and entered. Chad sat in front of a monitor.

He looked up. "Waiting to let dinner in. When the van stops at the gate, I punch this button. Hope you like pizza."

'I do. Tomorrow Claire's bringing a pan of lasagna and a jar of gravy for chicken parm on

Sunday. Which room will be mine?"

He grinned. 'You can share with me."

"Chad."

"The one next to mine. We'll share a bathroom. Mine is the end room on the right."

She picked up the bag. "I need to shower and get out of my work clothes." He started to turn the chair. "Dinner. I can find the room."

"Got you. They're here. See you soon."

Emma found the room. She stripped and quickly showered. As the water sprayed over her from a number of jets, she laughed. She could get used to this.

She returned to the main room and found the pizza box on the table. She and Chad carried slices on plates to watch the news while they ate. When they finished she put the leftovers away.

"What now?" Chad asked.

She walked to the window. "No walk. The promised rain has arrived." Thunder rumbled. Jagged lines of lightning shot across the dark sky.

"A movie? Talk? Cards?"

She sat close enough to catch his hand. "We'll start with talk. How is yours and Rob's project coming?"

"We signed for the place. Met with an architect and contractor. Work will begin next week." He laughed. "I've been ordering equipment and reaching out to some people I know who might be willing to come aboard."

"That's good." She wanted to believe this

would happen and the movie would make millions and Chad would remain in Fern Lake. But that was for the future and this was now.

Chad tugged on her hand. "And you. How did your day go?"

"Nothing special happened."

"Do you ever get tired of the routine?"

She shook her head. "The patients need me. Sometimes I encounter a puzzle to solve. That's fun." The way they approached work was another of their differences.

"Movie or cards?" he said.

"Movie. I'll pop corn."

"I don't know where any could be."

She hurried to her room and returned waving a packet. "Microwave."

"I like the way you think."

She joined him and sat on a chair beside his wheelchair. They flipped on the TV and hunted for a movie both would enjoy. She opened the bag of popcorn. "What to drink?"

"Soda. This is our first date in a long time."

Once they were settled he began the movie. They watched, shared popcorn and kisses. Though she wanted to keep part of her aloof, Emma found herself becoming aroused.

Should have known this would happen.

He tugged her onto his lap. The kisses grew heated. The rain continued. The clock chimed eleven times. Chad straightened. "Jeff will be here soon."

Emma slid from his lap and cleared away the drinks and popcorn. The doorbell rang and the door opened. A tall young man with sandy hair entered the house.

"Jeff, good to see you. This is Emma."

"Hi." Jeff smiled. "Glad to meet you oficially. Saw you when I was his bodyguard."

"Me, too. Chad says you were a medic. Why the career change?"

"I wanted something different. Too much tragedy as a medic." Jeff turned to Chad. "Ready to hit the sack?"

"I am." He wheeled away.

Emma went into the kitchen and checked the refrigerator for breakfast preparations. She filled the well of the coffee maker. She thought about getting ready for bed but she wasn't sure. She felt as worried as a teenager not knowing what to do.

Jeff returned. "He's all set. I'll be here tomorrow at eight. Let me show you how to set the night system. You'll have to disengage in the morning before I arrive. Hope you weren't planning to sleep in."

"I'll be leaving not long after you arrive. I've rounds to make at the hospital."

He showed her what to do. She practiced several times. Then she watched the monitor until he drove through the gates. She set the alarm and went to tell Chad good night.

When she entered his room, he smiled the body melting smile. "Come here," he said. "You're not getting away."

She went to the bed. He kissed her. His hands slid beneath her top and he unfastened her bra. "I want you. I have for weeks."

The kiss deepened and she felt the throbbing need for him. What harm would a time or two do? She wasn't committing herself to a forever and neither was he. She knew this wouldn't last. In a month or two he would return to Hollywood. Though he had his plans for making a move he would become again the man she'd read about.

She pulled back. "Give me a moment or two to change out of these clothes."

He stroked her breasts. They reacted. "Promise you'll return."

She stroked her chest. "I'll be back before you can count to a thousand." She pulled free and ran to the door. Behind her, she heard him count.

She dashed into the room where her things were and stripped. She pulled on the nightie she'd brought. Silk, bright blue, thin strapped and barely covering her bottom. She returned and heard him say nine hundred. Her eyes widened.

He had pulled off the cover and lay in nude splendor. His heavy erection lay on his abdomen. Her mouth dried and she slowly walked toward the bed.

"You look delicious," he said. "Condoms in the top drawer. I brought a few. One never knows."

She opened the drawer and laughed. "Only a few. There must be several dozen." She lifted several and approached the bed.

"Closer," he drawled.

She winked and kissed him. She sat on the edge of the bed. "Close enough."

"No,"

She moved until her legs were on either side of his thighs. He ran a hand beneath her short nightie and sucked in a breath. "I do like what you're wearing."

"Do you now?" She leaned forward. "I like what you're not wearing." Her lips touched his.

He stroked her rear and grasped the hem of the nightgown. Their lips parted and tongues touched and tasted. She lifted her head to take a breath and kissed her way over his stubbled chin. She licked his neck and moved down on her way to explore more of his body.

Emma." His guttural cry caused her to stop. She looked and saw the desire in his eyes and moved so she no longer straddled him. With slow strokes, her hands massaged his chest and down his abdomen to circle his erection. She opened the condom. Before rolling the sheath over him, her tongue darted out to touch the tip.

"You're driving me crazy," he growled.

She grasped him and slowly slid the condom over his erection. He grasped her hips and pulled her over him. He used his hands to stroke her breasts. When he rolled her nipples with his fingers, she felt a throbbing in her core.

She sank down to sit on his thighs. "Emma, please." She leaned forward and kissed him. Slowly she slid over him. When he was deep inside her, she paused to let her body adjust to his size.

He ran his hands over her torso and slipped a finger to touch her. The stimulation caused her to rock. He flexed his hips and met her rocking body. They erupted like a volcano spewing. Their bodies shook with the after quakes.

She collapsed on his chest. His arms wrapped around her. "I love you, love you, love you."

His words vibrated through her. He paused as though waiting for her to speak. She couldn't. To say anything would reveal how deeply he'd embedded himself into her life.

Chapter 9

The rising sun and the dipping mattress woke Chad. He rolled on his side and saw Emma reach for her nightie. "Good morning."

She gasped. "I tried to let you sleep."

"Why are you up so early?"

"It's quarter after seven. I want to shower and dress before Jeff arrives. I'll make breakfast for us before I leave for the hospital."

He grinned. "Come here."

She paused beside the bed. He pulled her down so he could kiss her. His hands grasped her waist and tugged her onto the bed. She pressed her hands against his chest. "Save this for later. I really need to go."

He released her. "Until tonight."

She nodded. "After rounds I'll go home to help Claire with the housework. I'll bring Brian and her back along with a pan of lasagna for tonight, a container of gravy and fixings for chicken parm on Sunday."

"I'll be waiting."

She walked to the door. He watched the hemline of her nightie reveal glimpses of her buttocks. He felt his cock swell with anticipation. Not until tonight. This thought didn't quell the desire pulsing through his veins.

He clutched the sheet and wished the casts away. A fool's dream. One couldn't return to the past and make changes. He groaned. This was just another hit of fate.

At eight Jeff arrived. Before long Chad had showered and dressed for the day. He followed Jeff down the hall. Emma stood at the stove. She turned. "Jeff, would you join us for breakfast?"

"Not today. I'm meeting Simon. We're designing security for the studio."

"Another step closer to the opening," Chad said. "Thanks for the news. I know how I'll spend a few hours today. I'm going shopping."

Emma carried plates to the table. Chad joined her. He took a bite of the fluffy omelet. "Delicious." He savored the flavors of ham, cheese and tomatoes. He lifted a glass of orange juice and toasted Emma. "How did you make this so fluffy?"

"I whipped the whites." She poured coffee for both and sat to eat.

"I must tell Rob. His omelets are good but not like this."

When they finished, she cleaned the table and counters. "I'm off to the hospital. I'll see you around two this afternoon. There's leftover pizza for lunch. Heat it in the microwave."

"Will do." He clasped her hand. "You're not leaving without a kiss or two."

She laughed and lightly touched his lips with hers. "Until later."

The temptation to kiss her until they finished what they'd started this morning took hold. He couldn't. He must get used to patients needing her. "See you later."

He spent the rest of the morning creating lists of names of potential employees and salaries. He also studied the script and listed the characters with thoughts of who he might convince to take the roles of the three female characters.

At noon, he zapped the pizza and ate the two remaining slices. He had just finished when he heard the doorbell. He went to the door and let Emma, Claire and Brian in.

The dark haired boy grinned. "Aunt Emma and Mom said you were a movie star."

"I am."

"I couldn't tell my friends at school about you." He studied the casts. "How come no one wrote on them?"

"No one asked."

"Could I?"

"Sure, but I don't know where there are any markers."

The boy looked at his mother. She reached into the huge purse she carried and handed him a package. "Here you are."

Chad laughed. "Amazing. Are you prepared for everything?"

"Close to. A mother's survival kit for those times when boredom or restlessness strikes."

Brian opened the pack and chose a color. He printed his name.

Emma carried a huge canvas bag into the kitchen. She loaded a number of containers into the fridge. She winked. "That's for dinner."

"Can we swim now?" Brian patted Chad's cast. "Bet you wish you could swim."

"You're so right. With luck it won't be long before I can."

"What will you do while we're swimming? Won't you get bored?"

Chad laughed. "I'll ask your mom for something from the magic bag. I'll watch you swim so you can show me all you've learned." He started down the path to the pool. Brian pulled off his shirt and sandals.

"Wait for us." Emma's clothes joined Brian's on a chair.

Chad admired the way her one piece suit hugged her body. His hands itched to caress the curves. Last night had been great but his body pulsed with need. Today would be long.

Brian jumped into the pool. "Watch me." He swam across the shallow end. "I did it. This is farther than I ever swam at school."

Chad clapped. "Before long you'll be able to swim to the diving board and back." His thoughts centered on what might have been. If he hadn't neglected Emma and kept the lines of communication open to push for closeness, they could have married and had a son by now.

He groaned. Dwelling on regrets brought nothing but sadness.

After an hour in the pool, Emma stretched out on a chaise. Chad settled his wheelchair beside her. "Brian is a great kid. Where is his father?"

"Far from here, I hope."

His forehead wrinkled. 'Why?"

"Long story."

"Tell me."

"Claire met Kevin in college. He convinced her to drop out and work. She did. He continued at school until he earned a MBA. She got pregnant, had Brian and continued to work. Kevin had a roving eye and a heavy hand. She put up with this until the night he hit her and Brian tried to stop him and he slammed the child into a wall."

"Sorry to hear that. She's better out of the relationship."

"They're both recovering, with help." She sucked in a breath. "If he stays away they'll be fine." She rolled on her stomach.

Chad closed his eyes. How could a man beat his wife and harm his son? His admiration for Claire grew. He would be glad to have her for a sister. All he had to do was convince Emma to marry him.

Emma stretched and rose. "I'm heading to the house to start dinner." She pulled on her shorts and top. "The lasagna will need oven time."

Though he could have followed her, he brought the wheelchair to the side of the pool and watched Brian bating a huge ball and then swimming after it."

"Where's Emma?" Claire asked.

145

"Making dinner."

She paused at the side of the pool. "Brian, come out and dry yourself. Time to help your aunt with dinner."

A short time later, Chad followed the pair up the path to the cabin. When he opened the door, the aroma of garlic filled the air. His stomach growled. Emma stood at the stove doing something to a loaf of bread. Claire and Brian took vegetables from the refrigerator.

"What can I do?" Chad asked.

"Show Brian where the silverware and paper napkins are. Then you can take drink orders. There's iced tea and iced coffee ready."

Before long they sat at the table. Chad took a bite of the lasagna. "This is wonderful."

"Thanks," Claire said. "It's easy to make."

They finished dinner and went for a walk. Then they returned to the living room to watch a movie while they ate cannoli.

Brian yawned. Claire rose. "Emma, he needs to go home."

Emma nodded. "I'm coming." She turned to Chad. "I'll see you later. Save my cannoli." She grabbed her shoulder bag and followed her sister and nephew outside.

After they left he turned off the television. Would she return? If she chose not to that would be fitting. He sat near the window and stared at the moon. When he saw her car he relaxed. He switched on the TV, No sense letting her know how much he wanted her. They couldn't do much until Jeff had come and left.

146

* * *

On Tuesday Emma left to make rounds. She thought of the time spent with Chad. There had been much talk, enough so they seemed to be on their old footing. There'd also been the best sex she'd ever experienced. Her emotions remained mixed. She admitted to herself she still loved him but she didn't trust this to last. Not completely. She returned to her routine.

For the next two weeks, she spent only a few evenings with him.

On the last Wednesday in July, Emma joined Chad for dinner. "Your casts should be off soon."

He nodded. "I have an appointment with Dr. Markham next week. He wants X-rays." He scowled. "Means I have to go to the hospital for them. I'm sure someone will tell the press and they will come."

Emma straightened. "I have an idea you could run past Markham. Manon rents the basement of our offices to a radiologist. There's an entrance with a ramp from the parking lot. I imagine he can do the X-rays."

He reached for his cell and laughed. "Can't call this evening but I will tomorrow.' He kissed her hand. "Thanks."

She laughed. "Let me know when and I'll come down and help you onto the table."

"Will do."

They waved to Rob and Andi and went

outside to walk. They stopped at their usual place. The sultry summer night settled around them. "You'll soon be cast free. What then?"

"A ton of physical therapy to regain my strength. I'll do as much as I can here. Rob knows a physical therapist who'll come to the house."

Emma closed her eyes and listened to the rustling leaves. Soon the time would end and he would return to his old life. An ache built in her chest. She bit her lower lip. No tears. She had always known this wouldn't last. She needed to distance herself.

The next evening when she reached the cabin, Chad clasped her hands. "Talked to Markham this morning. He's happy about the X-ray. I'm scheduled for Monday at ten AM. With luck, I'll return on Wednesday without these casts."

"I'll keep my fingers crossed."

He pulled her close for a heated kiss. She swallowed. She refused to cry.

On Monday morning Emma had scheduled her patients so she could help with Chad from the wheelchair onto the examining table. Rob and Simon arrived with Chad and Jeff. Jeff took the lead. He had placed a folded sheet on the chair to be used as a lift.

"Simon and I will use the lift sheet. Emma, can you do the legs? Rob, you'll need to put your arms under his. When I count to three, we'll lift."

Emma took her place at the foot of the

wheelchair. She slid her arms under the casts. Jeff stood on the far side of the table and grasped the end of the sheet. Simon and Rob took their places.

"On the count," Jeff said. "One. Two. Three."

Surprisingly the transfer went smoothly. As the radiologist placed the plates beneath Chad's legs, he ordered the others from the room.

Emma chuckled. "Teamwork at its best."

"And we only have to do this once more," Rob said. "I hope Wednesday really happens for him."

On Wednesday afternoon, Chad called. "I'm free."

"No casts. That's great," Emma said.

"There's a brace for the left leg and two canes." He groaned. "I managed to stand for a few seconds. The physical therapist will be here soon to start exercises."

"You'll do fine."

"Come to dinner tonight. To celebrate."

"Will do."

When Emma finished office hours, she hurried home. The dog days of August had arrived. She dressed in shorts and a sleeveless shirt. After telling Claire and Brian good evening, she drove to Rob's. When she used the number at the gate nothing happened. She tried again.

She reached for her cell. The moment she heard Chad's voice, she spoke. "The gate numbers didn't work."

"Sorry. I'll open the gate for you. Evidently the numbers are changed every month."

"Interesting."

"I'll give you the new code after I twist Rob's arm."

The gate opened. Emma drove through and parked in the circle. Andi and Tammy waited near the path to the pool. "We're eating out tonight. Rob's grilling chicken and corn on the cob. Summer's my favorite time. There are also great tomatoes."

"Where's Chad?"

"In the pool. The therapist came this afternoon and gave him some exercises for the pool as well as in his room." She shook her head. "He's trying for instant recovery."

"Sounds like him. He was like that as a teen when he set out to learn all kinds of martial art systems. That was beside his studies, track, part-time jobs and the local theater. I doubt he slept more than four hours a night."

When they reached the pool area, Emma pulled a chaise to the poolside and watched Chad. He stood in the shallow end and braced one arm on the edge of the pool. He slowly walked forward. When he reached the end, he turned and started back.

He paused at the area where she sat. "I have another round to complete. Did you bring your suit?"

She shook her head. "Never thought to do that."

"Then I'll continue alone."

When he finished the next tour, he pulled himself onto the edge. She watched his arm muscles bunch. "Now you have to watch while I stand. It's not a pretty sight."

Emma stood. "I'll help."

"I need the wheelchair and the thing."

"What thing?"

"It's a triangle that looks like steps."

Emma left to find the sort of ladder. Andi steered the wheelchair toward Chad. Tammy sat in the seat. "I ride," the toddler exclaimed.

Emma laughed. "Looks like you do." She found the contraption and carried it to where Chad now knelt. He put his hands on the third step. As he moved his hands from step to step, he began to stand. Andi pushed the wheelchair behind him. He sank onto the seat."

"How's dinner coming?" he called. "I'm starved."

Emma pointed to where Rob waved a huge fork. "Looks like food is ready." She walked beside the chair to the wooden table set beneath an awning. Chad stopped the chair at the end. She slid onto a bench beside him. "How are you?"

"Impatient. There are parallel bars in my room. I'll show you later." He touched her hand. "My sense of balance is messed up. I feel like a toddler except Tammy walks better than I can. Then there's the brace."

She met his gaze. "You've been castless for a few hours. Be patient."

Chad's grip on her hand tightened. "I've

little of that. I have plans I want to put in motion. I need to return, sell my house and hire some people who could make the movie work."

Emma laughed. How much he sounded like the teenage boy who had constantly spoken of his plans for Hollywood and stardom. He had achieved those goals. Perhaps his new ones would be reached.

Would he stay in Fern Lake or would making Rob's book into a movie catapult him into a new path to fame? If that happened, he would head for California. Their time together was ending. She would again face the loss of him, this time forever.

He lifted her hand and kissed the palm ,closing her fingers over the mark. She drew a deep breath and prayed for a life with him. Deep inside, she knew the dream would again be forgotten.

Chad tugged on her hand. "Why the wrinkled brow?"

She shrugged. "Just thinking of the future."

"And that worries you?"

How could she respond? She wanted no more promises he would break. "I'm not sure."

"Emma, I love you. We'll have the life we've planned."

"Will we?"

"I love you. Do you love me?"

"I do but...I loved you years ago. Then I hated you. I can't think beyond the day you stopped calling."

"I've changed. You'll see."

She couldn't be sure. At the moment he planned to stay in Fern Lake but he had to return to Hollywood where temptation abounded. She bent and kissed him. Dare she hope?

* * *

Chad settled back. He must find a way to persuade Emma he had changed. He loved her. He wanted to live with her forever. To achieve that meant a quick trip to Hollywood to sell the house, deal with Gregson and return. To make that happen he had to build his strength and convince her to come with him. She would be the perfect buffer against his agent and his promo ops. That was the plan.

For the next two weeks he worked as hard as he could. He even persuaded his friends to help him with extra time on the parallel bars.

One afternoon Dr. Markham made a house call. "I'm pleased with your progress."

"Can I travel to California to take care of business?"

"When you can walk with a single cane."

Those words produced a goal. As the days of August moved forward, he worked harder.

As Labor Day neared, he and Emma walked along the path near the pool. When they reached the clearing he sank on the bench. Emma sat beside him.

Chad released a held breath. "That's the farthest I've walked. Another week and I'll be ready to move ahead."

"I'm glad you're improving."

He pulled her into an embrace and kissed her. "I've got to deal with matters in California. Has your partner returned to work yet?"

"She has."

"Then you can take time off and come with me."

She shook her head. "I can't."

"Why not?"

"Manon is only there for half days until September. The doctor who helped out is away until sometime after Labor Day. Not sure exactly when but he'll work while I go on vacation."

He scowled. "I want to finish as quickly as I can so I can return and start production."

Emma pulled back. 'I have my responsibilities. I can't just take off on a whim. Being in practice is my life. I'm not about to give it up."

His expression turned so glum she wanted to comfort him. She couldn't toss her life away. She'd spent too much time developing her skills. Whether he stayed or not she had to keep her obligations.

Chad stared at his hands. Was this the end? He clasped her hand. "I love you. I don't want to be away from you for weeks."

She paused and he knew what she wanted to say. She wanted to bring up the past and how he had disappointed her.

Days later he walked using one cane. He wore the leg brace for long distances. Simon had smuggled him into the studio. He's seen the alterations being made and had unpacked some boxes of equipment. The security system was state of the art. He set his plans for the trip.

He had Simon ease him into the jewelry store. He spent an hour choosing a ring for Emma. A ruby in the center and a pair of onyx for the sides.

In three days Labor Day would be celebrated. He had reserved a room at a local upscale hotel using his alias. The jeweler promised the ring would be delivered that afternoon.

At five on Labor Day, Chad waited for Emma to arrive for their stay at the hotel. His body pulsed with an eagerness to be alone with her. When he saw her car crest the rise, he grinned.

Rob turned from the stove. "Good luck."

"I'll need all I can find." With one overnight case in hand and his cane in the other, he left the house. Emma stepped from her car. Chad's mouth went dry. The dress she wore caressed her curves the way he wanted to stroke her body.

She opened the trunk. He tossed his bag inside. Before she stepped away he pulled her into his arms. "I've been waiting for this seems like forever." He brushed his lips over hers.

She winked. "Why stand here? Let's go."

"Right." He put on his dark glasses and got into the car.

Emma slid into the driver's seat, fastened

her seatbelt and started the car. "Seems silly going to a hotel in town."

"Can you think of an alternative? Here or at your place there are people."

She nodded. "Curious ones."

"If you would come with me we could have every night and most days."

She laughed. "We could also have flashing cameras and more reporters dogging us."

He nodded. "You're right but think of the fun we could have."

She paused at the gates. "I really have no desire to be featured in the tabloids."

"I understand. They won't be so greedy for gossip when they learn Storm is dead."

Before long they reached the hotel and parked in the underground lot. They rode the elevator to the main floor and checked in. Chad used his Ian Greve identification. They rode the elevator to the top level. Once inside their room, Emma unpacked their bags.

Chad walked onto the balcony and sat at the table set for their meal. Back inside, he mixed a rum and cola for himself and opened the refrigerator to find the frozen lime daiquiri he'd ordered for Emma. They carried their drinks to the large balcony and sat on a chaise.

He slid an arm around her and snugged her close. "Nice view."

She nodded. "I'm not sure how they managed to buy property overlooking the lake."

"Money," he said. "Rob's family owned the land. He sold most of the properties."

"I know. He was obsessed with repaying the people his father and brother cheated. That's how my dad and a few of his friends could move to Florida." She sipped her drink.

Chad leaned over and ran his lips over hers. Though he wanted to devour her, that must wait. He heard the buzzer and struggled to his feet. "I believe dinner is served."

He walked to the door. A series of carts and a waiter were there. The man arrived and placed the first course on the table. Chad seated Emma.

The meal began with shrimp cocktails. A clear broth followed, then a salad. The main course was a succulent salmon dish. Coffee accompanied the meal. The waiter presented the deserts, a luscious cherry torte.

Chad turned to Emma. "Shall we save this for later?"

She nodded. "Another bite and I won't be able to move from the table."

The waiter placed the dessert in the refrigerator. He pushed the last cart to the door.

Chad rose and led Emma into the sitting room. He flicked a switch. Music flowed from hidden speakers. He drew her into his arms. "Now for a test of my abilities. Let's dance."

She moved closer and put her arms around his neck. He clasped her waist. At first they moved to the music. Before long they did little more than sway.

She raised her head and stared into his eyes. He saw desire in their dark depths. His mouth met hers. She opened for his exploration. His heart thundered. His cock filled and urgent need arose. Emma moved against him with growing urgency.

Chad released her lips. "I love you. I need you."

"I need you, too."

He found the tab of the zipper down the back of her dress. She opened the buttons on his shirt. As he pushed the dress from her shoulders, she unfastened his belt and unbuttoned his trousers. He cupped her breasts. The wish to savor every inch of her skin warred with the desire to possess her.

Slowly they walked to the bedroom. Chad pulled a strip of condoms from the dresser. He finished stripping.

Emma laughed. "Intending to use them all?"

"Perhaps."

She removed her bra and bikini. She cut the distance between them. Her breasts pressed against his chest. He felt her nipples tighten. "I'm ready to fly." She lay on the bed.

Chad joined her. He ran his hand over her skin and watched the way her eyes reacted to the caresses. Her little gasps and the quivers thrilled him. He sheathed himself and bent to kiss her. As he slid into her the kiss deepened. Slowly he sped his pace and as she climaxed he followed.

He gathered her into his arms and held her close. Kisses and caresses brought them to a calm place. "I love you."

"I love you," she echoed.

Chad reached onto the bedside stand and opened the box. "Will you wear this and marry me?"

"It's beautiful."

He slid the ring onto her finger. "Will you?"

She drew a deep breath. "I will."

"When?"

She slipped the ring off. "I can't set a date or accept the ring. You must take care of your business in Hollywood. Ask me again when you return."

Though what she said hurt, he couldn't blame her. He had abandoned her years ago. He slipped the ring into the box and kissed her.

"I love you and in less than a month, I'll be back." He held her close. "Now where were we?"

She responded to him with fervor. Hope soared.

Chapter 10

Three days after Labor Day Emma reached Rob's house where Chad waited to load his duffle into the trunk. Today he returned to Hollywood. She swallowed a sigh. Would he resist falling into his old lifestyle? Her worries about his failure tightened her throat. At the moment she wished her obligations to her patients weren't an imperative.

He settled in the front seat. "Morning." He leaned over to kiss her. "Time to go." She sank back in the seat.

As she started the car, Rob left the house. He paused beside Chad's open window. "Hurry back. We have a new world to conquer."

Chad laughed. "With luck I'll be back in two weeks."

"Then the games begin." Rob clasped Chad's hand. "See you soon."

Emma drove down the winding drive, exited the gate and turned toward the local airport twenty miles from town. She couldn't think of anything to say. She couldn't beg him to stay. He had loose ends to settle in order to face the drastic changes he planned to make. Could he? She wished she could be sure.

They reached the small airport. A jet waited on the runway. She carried Chad's duffle and walked beside him to the plane. She handed the bag to the steward.

Chad held her in an embrace. "I'll finish my business as soon as I can and come straight back." He tilted her chin and kissed her.

Warmth chased some of the chill she felt. "When you do, we'll talk."

"I love you," he said. "That won't change."

"I love you, too." She did but her fears of how he would react to temptation held sway.

Using his cane Chad climbed the steps. In the doorway he paused and blew a kiss. "Two or three weeks and I'll be back. I'll call every night and report my progress."

"I'll be waiting." After blowing him a kiss she turned and strode to the car. She watched until the plane vanished. A few tears trickled over her cheeks. She wiped her eyes and slid into the driver's seat. He was gone. Though she believed he would return to make the movie, she doubted he could back away from his role as Storm. So much of his life had been invested in those movies.

He loves you. He said he wouldn't abandon you again. She had to cling to his promise to keep memories of the past at bay.

She started the car and drove home. She hadn't lost him yet. Trust and belief must be ever present. She strode into the kitchen.

Claire turned from the stove. "Fried chicken and baked potatoes for dinner. Flight go all right?"

"Absolutely. Where's Brian?"

"Brad Markham picked him up to go swimming with Jamie and Amy. They'll be back for dinner."

Emma arched an eyebrow. "Something happening there?"

Claire shook her head. "I'm not ready for anything."

Emma opened the fridge and gathered some lemons to make a pitcher of lemonade. She checked the iced tea and noticed a nearly full pitcher and one of iced coffee. She poured a glass of the coffee and added some cream. Carrying the drink she went upstairs to change into shorts. She pushed all thoughts of Chad away.

When she returned to the kitchen, Claire began frying the chicken. "Are you really okay?"

"He said he'd come back. I have to trust him."

"Why didn't you go with him? I'm sure he asked."

"The patients. Manon is working just part-time. Dr. Reid is out of town."

"Are you all right with him being out there alone?"

"I have to be. I look on this as a test. He said he would be back in two of three weeks."

"And if he doesn't return then?"

Emma popped potatoes in the microwave. "If he isn't back, I'll be on a two week's singles' cruise."

Claire laughed. "Sounds like a plan."

* * *

Chad slept for most of the flight except for eating an excellent meal. When the plane landed the steward helped him descend the steps and walked with him to where the limo waited. He gave his address and they set off. So far no one had learned about his return. He hadn't told his agent. Gregson hadn't called today.

When they reached the gate of the estate, Chad used the opener on his key ring to let the limo enter. He hobbled into the house. The air smelled stale. After switching on the cooling system he walked to the kitchen. Was there anything to eat in the house?

In the freezer, he found a frozen meal from one of his favorite restaurants. He zapped the food in the microwave. Tomorrow he had to drive somewhere for breakfast except...he had no car.

Though he regretted the need, after he ate, he hit Gregson's number. "Chad here."

"Where are you?"

"At home."

"I'll come over and we'll discuss our next move. I think we can force the studio to pay you more for Storm films."

Chad groaned. "That's not up for negotiations. Come in the morning. You can take me to breakfast and to shop for some food.

I'm selling the house. When we go on this expedition remember I need to be here at one to speak to the realtor."

"I'll be there around ten. If I'd known you were coming today I would have met the plane."

"See you tomorrow." Chad figured he could hold out until ten. There were a dozen or more pods of coffee. He called the realtor and scheduled the appointment for one. Then he wandered from room to room deciding what furniture he would take and wondering what to do with the rest.

* * *

On Monday Emma made hospital rounds and drove to the office. As she prepared to see patients she wondered about Chad. When he'd called last evening, he'd sounded tired.

Manon entered, carrying the baby in his car seat.

"Is he staying?" Emma asked.

Manon shook her head. "The sitter's due to arrive soon."

Emma crouched and amused the infant. When the sitter arrived, Emma hurried to her office and slipped on her lab coat. The arrival of patients kept her from thinking about Chad but she couldn't help wondering if his agent had arrived and what the realtor would say about the house.

At lunch, Manon gestured for Emma to come into her office. "I understand Chad left.

Why didn't you go with him?"

"I couldn't. You're only working half days. My leaving would have been bad for the patients and the practice."

"I think you were foolish. He says he loves you. What if he becomes involved in a movie and decides to stay?"

Emma set her sandwich down. "This is a test. Years ago he made promises he didn't keep."

Manon nodded. "I know about broken promises. Why didn't you fly out there back then and learn what went on?"

"I saw why. On television. In the tabloids. Why would I go there when he thrived on his new life and forgot me?"

Manon shrugged. "It's your life. Just don't give up too soon."

* * *

As promised, Gregson arrived at ten. While waiting, Chad drank four cups of coffee and ate stale crackers he'd found. After a late breakfast they went to a local market where Chad purchased cold cuts, rolls and a few easy to prepare foods. Cameras flashed. People snapped pictures with their cell phones. Chad cringed. Welcome back to a normality he no longer wanted. Though he'd mentioned leasing a car, Gregson ignored him.

At the house Chad stored his purchases. "I'm good for a week. I really need to rent a car."

"No reason to do that," Gregson said. "I'm glad to chauffer you. I've booked us for dinner tonight. We need to talk about the contracts." He paused. "Can you walk without the cane?"

Chad grasped the marble hand grip. "For short distances." He pulled up his left pant leg. "There's this, too." Though he really didn't need the brace, its presence added to his reason for killing Storm.

"Will you need that forever?"

"I don't know." He glanced at the clock. "I'll see you later. The realtor is due soon."

Gregson walked to the door. "I'm sorry you're selling this place. I'll keep my eyes open for a smaller one. Maybe on the beach."

"Not here." Chad's hands fisted. "I'm returning to Fern Lake. I've a movie to make." *And a woman to claim.*

Gregson laughed. "We'll see about that. After a few days here you'll change your mind. I'll be here at six thirty. We'll have dinner and talk. It's not a casual place."

When the door closed Chad strode to the kitchen and made a sandwich. Memories of Rob's gourmet meals and Emma's red sauce made the sandwich taste like cardboard. He bit and chewed. He wouldn't eat like this forever.

The realtor arrived and Chad toured the house and pointed out the furniture he intended to take, mainly his bedroom and the sound system. She said having most of the rooms furnished might provide sales appeal. What the buyer didn't want could be sold. He agreed.

Once she left he napped. At five he showered and dressed for dinner. Wearing a tie after two months of not seemed odd. He met Gregson at the door.

When they reached the restaurant he faced a barrage of flashes. Questions were shouted but he gave no comment. Inside they were escorted to a table in a secluded corner.

Gregson pulled papers from his briefcase. "I need you to sign for Storm five."

Chad scanned the papers. "I told you I'm done with Storm. Doctor's orders."

"They want you for at least three scenes. One with Lightning, one with the attempt on your life and one other."

Chad drew a deep breath. "I can do those but…"

"They would consider distributing the movie you want to make."

The dangling carrot made him want to jump. "When will they start shooting?"

"I don't know. Just sign so I can speak to them about dates."

Chad's lips tightened. "I have a schedule I need to keep. I said I'd be gone two or three weeks."

"I'll let them know."

Chad scrawled his signature in the places where needed. He looked up. Two leggy blondes sauntered toward the table. He looked for an escape and found no way to avoid the women.

They stopped at the table. "Chad Morgan," one of the women drawled. "I thought it was you. Where have you been?"

"And your rainmaker." The second blond caressed Gregson's shoulder.

"Join us for dessert." Gregson signaled the waiter. "Cheese cake and champagne."

Chad's hands fisted. Another photo op arranged. He rolled his eyes. How to vanish? He definitely had to rent a car.

The tallest blonde slid closer to him. "After dessert, let's go to a club."

"I'm not into clubbing these days."

She turned to Gregson. "Are you on?"

"Absolutely." Gregson glared at Chad. "Clubbing is a great way to let everyone know you're back."

Chad shook his head. He would find a way out as soon as he could. He passed on the champagne but ate his slice of cheesecake.

As they left the restaurant, they faced a cluster of cameras. A young reporter thrust a microphone in Chad's face. "Chad Morgan, where have you been? Are you healed from your accident?"

He waved the cane. "Mostly."

"When will you start filming the next Storm flick?"

"I haven't a clue."

The valet opened the car door. The tall blonde pushed him into the rear seat. Before he could stop her, she wrapped her arms around him. Light from flashbulbs lit the interior of the car. Chad reached for his phone. If Emma saw the picture she would believe he'd reverted.

He untangled himself. "Gregson, take these ladies to where they want to go. Then take me home."

The agent laughed. "And give up the opportunity for another photo op? I've arranged for an interview at the club. My friend, you're back."

"Not on a bet."

When the car stopped at the club's valet stand, Chad used his phone and called a cab. "I'm going home."

"You can't," Gregson said. "Being here is important for your image."

"Maybe yours. Not mine." The blonde clung to his arm. He peeled her fingers away. "I'm not interested."

She turned and sneered. "You're nothing. Gregson had to beg me to come."

A cab pulled to the curb. Chad got in. After giving the address, he hit Emma's number. He had to talk to her.

* * *

"Emma," Claire called. "You have to come now."

Wondering what emergency had occurred, Emma dashed downstairs. Had Brian done something? Had Kevin appeared on their doorstep? She entered the living room in time to hear the TV host of Hollywood Chatters speak.

169

"With his bad boy flair, Chad Morgan is back."

Pictures followed. Chad at breakfast with his agent. Chad shopping in a market. Chad being kissed by a flashy blonde. Not a quick kiss but a long and lingering one.

"Here's the latest scoop. Chad Morgan and Storm are gearing up for a new flick. Filming begins sometime this month. Great news for his fans. Who will be his new heroine?"

Emma's eyes narrowed. She wasn't upset about the photos. Last night Chad had called and told her about Gregson's photo ops and how he had deserted the party to return home via a taxi. There had been other things he'd told her. The realtor's visit, the need to hire a moving van and to find a storage facility in Fern Lake.

The disturbing news was the mention of the fifth Storm movie. Was that merely the reporter and Chad's agent passing on a rumor? He hadn't mentioned that last night.

Claire looked away from the program. "Didn't take him long to return to his old ways."

Emma patted her sister's shoulder. "He told me about the dinner, the blonde invasion and the pictures. He's unhappy with his agent. Chad left them at some club and returned home in a taxi. He's renting a car so he doesn't have to depend on Gregson."

"You're more forgiving that I would be."

"I've no reason to doubt him where other women are concerned." But she distrusted the mention of his return as Storm.

Just then, her cell chimed. The number on

the screen brought a smile. As she walked to the porch and sat on the swing, she answered. "How are things going?"

"Better. I rented a car. I met with some people about Rob's movie. They're interested in the venture."

"That's great." She sucked in a breath. "I need to know something."

He laughed. "I have no secrets from you."

"What about the mention of you doing Storm again. Are you?"

He groaned. "I was going to tell you that this evening. I must but it's only for two or three scenes. The studio agreed to help with the distribution of Rob's movie. That provides a wider range for us."

She settled back and started the swing moving. "What are the scenes?"

"One is with Storm's protégée. The second is with the attempt to kill Storm. The third I believe is a scene where I play a corpse."

"Then you should be ready to return soon."

"As far as I know."

She relaxed. He hadn't failed. She prayed nothing would happen to ruin his plans.

They talked a bit more. He tried to coax her into setting a wedding date. She fended off his attempts. "When you're back in Fern Lake we can set a date." She thought of the ring she hadn't accepted.

"I wish you would tell me when we'll wed."

"I told you no long distance romance. We

tried that once and it didn't work."

He groaned. "My fault. So where are you?"

"On the porch swing."

"Wish I was with you."

So did she but he would be here in less than two weeks. "Here's the number of the storage facility you wanted." She read them.

"I'll call them tomorrow. I never realized how much trouble a move would be."

"Especially when you have no place here."

He chuckled. "I'll find something after I arrive. Talk to you tomorrow after I speak to Gregson and the producer and director. I intend to wear my brace."

She laughed. "And I remember how you disliked it. Take a copy of Dr. Markham's letter."

"I definitely will. I love you."

"And I love you."

The rest of the first week passed quickly with nightly phone calls. He told her about the picture and interviews he'd had. Then came the call that turned her life around. "I don't believe what happened. They won't start filming for another two weeks."

"That's dreadful."

"It's worse. I'll be on location. Is that doctor back yet?"

"No."

"You could fly out and see me."

"I'll think about that."

"They're dragging some doctor to examine me. They want the scene with my protégée to be

172

an action one."

The next evening on Hollywood Chatters, she received a shock. Chad was shown dancing with a gorgeous redhead.

"In the past day or two, Chad and Valerie have become quite the item. Rumors says her character and Storm's will wed. Will that hold true in real life?"

On the woman's left hand, a huge diamond flashed. Emma's breath caught. How would Chad explain this?

Her phone chimed. Chad's number flashed. She considered not answering but she needed to hear what he had to say. "Hello."

"Emma, don't believe everything you see and hear."

"As in…"

"Hollywood Chatters. Gregson and the studio set up the pictures. We were not dancing. They combined two photos."

For the next four days, the reports continued. Though Emma tried to have faith, she heard a strain in his voice when he called. Her spirits tumbled.

Why wouldn't he favor Valerie? Beside her, Emma felt as dull as a mud hen. She was ordinary. Dark hair, dark eyes and a body that put on pounds if she didn't hit the gym every day.

Chad was handsome. He needed a beautiful woman. People would see her at his side and wonder about his taste.

With each day he was away her spirits sank

lower. The night he called to say he would be on location until early October stunned her. She realized a happy ever after with him had vanished. Could she believe him when he said the reception in the remote area where he would be based was sporadic?

An excuse. Valid or invented? Emma chewed on her lower lip. She had known their affair wouldn't last. He'd been lonely when he was here. He'd missed the beautiful woman who flattered him. The only connection she and Chad had been in the past.

At lunch the next day, Dr. Reid strode in. "I'm back." He waved at Emma. "Don't you deserve a vacation?"

"I do."

"Just let me know when," he said.

Manon grinned. "So you're California bound."

"Going there wouldn't make much sense." Emma rose. "He'll be on location for as long as two weeks."

"Where will you go?"

"I'll let you know when and where tomorrow. For now, patients are waiting. She knew what she would do. She would take that singles' cruise she'd wanted to take before Chad returned to Fern Lake.

Chapter 11

Chad strode past the cabin located somewhere in the Rockies. This was his fifth visit to the area. Storm's retreat was secluded, isolated and for the week or two of filming mostly out of touch with civilization. The tree-covered slopes climbed toward the snow-covered mountains.

Valerie appeared at his side. She ran a hand down his back to settle on his ass. She leaned closer. Her lips brushed his ear. "Don't you feel what I do?" She squeezed.

Chad jerked away. "I feel nothing except an eagerness to finish this scene and move on."

"Don't you feel the connection flowing between us? As the latest Storm's lady, being with you electrifies me. Spending those evenings with you before we came for the filming were…"

"Promo ops orchestrated by Gregson. I have one woman. She's not here. Believe me. She isn't you." And how he wished Emma was here.

"I can feel your body respond the way mine does."

He turned. "Not to you but to memories.

175

There's no way you and I will be anything beyond a forced connection for the movie."

She flipped strands of her red hair from her shoulders. "You're wrong."

"Don't believe everything you read."

She sashayed away giving her rear a wiggle. "You'll see."

Chad drew a deep breath of the cool mountain air. Why did people believe manufactured rumors? No telling what garbage Gregson was feeding the eager gossip mongers.

"Morgan, time." The director snagged the phone from Chad's hand. "You'll get this after the shoot."

Chad nodded. "Let's get this over with." He strode onto the porch of Storms' cabin.

"Action," the director yelled.

Chad whirled to stare at the door. James Gould stepped out. "Storm, I'm ready to prove myself. Give me all you've got."

With this the fight began. Lightning leaped over the porch railing. Chad followed. The chase began. Bits of physical action were interspersed with the advance toward the goal."

As Chad leaped into the clearing, his left leg buckled. An ache escalated into pain and beyond. He slumped to the ground.

"Cut," the director shouted.

Chad rubbed his calf. He couldn't do another bit of action today. A soak in the hot tub followed by ice packs and a massage were in order.

The director strode over. "When can you

resume the scene?"

Though he wanted to say never, Chad struggled to his feet. "Tomorrow. I need to handle this."

The director's eyes flashed anger. "Then we'll resume filming tomorrow but a have a good idea for a scene today."

All Chad could think about was the hot tub. "What?"

"A scene with you and Valerie in the hot tub with a lot of sexual play."

Chad shook his head. "Not in the contract. Not happening."

"I don't see why not. Will make your last scene more poignant."

"I'd rather have a love scene with a viper." It was bad enough to think about her character crying over his dead body. Chad limped down the hill to the cluster or trailers. He reached the hot tub and found Lightning soaking.

"Good fight. Sorry your leg gave out. Hate the thought of beginning again tomorrow."

"So do I." Chad lowered himself into the bubbling water. "Let's hope we can finish tomorrow."

James climbed out. "I'm off to do my anger and vow of revenge scene. Hope they make no more changes."

"So do I." Since he wasn't involved in the rest of the scenes, Chad relaxed. The ache in his leg eased. Slowly the muscles relaxed. When he finished he pulled on his clothes and walked to his trailer. He sank on the couch to fasten the brace. The door opened.

Valerie entered. "Why did you refuse to do a hot tub scene with me?"

Chad met her gaze. "No sex for me in this movie. Go after James. You and he can burn the sheets when he comforts you after Storm dies."

"But...but..."

"I mean what I said."

She glared. "Why? You have sex in every Storm flick."

"Do I?"

"I know what I saw."

"Perhaps." He'd only done the deed in the first Storm film. The others had been accomplished by the miracle of photography. He wished he hadn't done the first one. He still felt anger at himself for being persuaded.

Valerie wheeled and stomped out slamming the door. Chad stretched out and held his cell phone hoping for luck. He hit Emma's number. Nothing happened. No service. He clutched the phone. After he rested he would search for a place where he could connect the call. There was much he needed to tell her.

That afternoon and evening he had no luck in his search for a live spot. Hopefully their last conversation had quieted her fears.

Completing the scene with Lightning took three days. By the end he wanted to hammer something. When would he film the last scene so he could escape?

Near the end of the second week on location, Chad wanted to scream. He had finally received the changes in the murder attempt scene and for the final one. He faced the director. "I thought Storm died. Why have you made the ending so vague?"

"You might want Storm to return in case your other matter fails."

Chad groaned. "Not happening. My new direction is set. I have partners who are behind me."

"Do you really think you can direct?"

"I won't know until I try. I've taken courses. I've studied films and watched directors. I've even thought about different approaches to scenes."

"Good luck then. Now about the ending. It stays. Your fans might demand you return."

With three takes of each scene, he was done. Tomorrow he would leave.

As he packed to leave, Gregson arrived. "Chad, good to see you. Wait until you see how hard I've been working to keep your image in the public eyes."

Chad groaned. "What have you done?"

Gregson handed Chad some papers. "And here are some tapes of Hollywood Chatters."

Chad took the articles and scanned them. "How could you?"

"You need the promo so people know you're back. Watch a clip of two." He loaded them into a tablet.

When Chad saw the second clip from Hollywood Chatters, he grasped Gregson's arm. "Damn it. Do you know what you've done?"

"Gained you and Storm some great publicity. When they see you and Valerie in the hot tub scene, they'll have the pair of you at the altar."

"There is no hot tub scene." Chad rose. "Start a denial campaign at once. I am not and never will be interested in her."

"I can't do that."

"Don't you mean won't? I'll give you a day to issue a retraction."

Gregson pulled free. "See you in Hollywood."

"You certainly will not." Chad hurried to finish packing.

* * *

Emma stared at her phone. Why hadn't he called? Two weeks filming he'd said. Poor reception area. She wanted to hear the truth from him, not from those reports on Hollywood Chatters. Two weeks of silence had ended last night.

Though she'd fought to push those thoughts aside, she had given up. She stared at the suitcases. Two packed and one waiting for her to finish. Should she change her flight until tomorrow and arrive in time to make the sailing time? What good would that do? She lifted a dress and carefully folded the recently purchased garment. Finally she added the special evening gown, a slender tube in red with a slit on one side. She snapped the case closed and fitted the special tags provided by the cruise line on each case.

With one last try, she hit Chad's number. Once again there was nothing but dead silence. She didn't bother to leave a voice message. He hadn't responded to any of the others she had already sent. A veil of sadness covered her thoughts. With great determination, she grabbed the luggage and dragged them downstairs. She would enjoy the cruise. She would find a man who would erase the deadness she felt.

Manon and Claire sat in the living room. Brian played with the baby. Emma paused in the doorway. "I'm set."

Manon rose and hugged her. "I've all the info about the cruise in case I need to reach you about one of the patients. Have a great time and knock their eyes out." She grinned. "You're dressed for success."

Emma chuckled. "Thanks."

Manon lifted the car seat and walked to her car. Claire and Emma brought the bags. Brian skipped behind. Manon waved as she drove away. Once the suitcases were in the trunk and Brian in his car seat, Emma sat in the passenger's seat.

"Do you have everything? Tickets, reservations, driver's license and the confirmation?" Claire asked.

"And my passport. All here." Emma tapped her shoulder bag.

During the hour and a half drive to the international airport, Emma and Claire talked about everything but Chad. Brian chattered about school, Jamie and Amy. "Will you send me a postcard?"

"I will and I'll find a present or two."

"Goody."

Emma smiled. Life was so simple for a child. She pushed all thoughts aside of her complicated life and imagined the cruise and the men she would meet. Hopefully there would be one to interest her.

At the airport, she checked in her luggage and walked to the inspection line. After hugging Brian and Claire, she stood in the check-in line. She placed her carry-on, handbag, phone and shoes in a bin and entered the scanner. She arrived at the departure gate fifteen minutes before boarding began.

Two hours plus saw her to Miami. Hauling her luggage, she found the bus to the hotel where she would spend the night. She studied the other passengers. Were any of the men booked for the cruise? One or two looked interesting. When the bus reached the hotel, a woman drew those aside who were taking the cruise. She spoke of the schedule for the next morning. At eight thirty, they would board a bus for the ship and have time to settle in their rooms before the eleven AM departure time.

Emma settled in her room. At six she went to the bar for a drink. She noticed several women who had been at the short meeting. She joined them for dinner. Then she returned to her room to vegetate.

* * *

Chad finally coxed the rental car to start. The urge for speed filled him. He reached the small town at the foot of the hill and the local garage. The mechanic shook his head. "Be two days before I get the part."

The scream in Chad's throat erupted with a growl. "Can I rent a car?" he asked. "I need to be home tonight." He wasn't sure what spurred the urge to hurry. He felt if he didn't see the damage Gregson had set in motion finished all would be lost.

The mechanic looked up. "No rentals but for a price my brother will drive you. He could use the money. He has one more year of college."

Four hours later, Chad hit the gate opener on his key ring. At the door of the house, he handed the young man a wad of bills. "Thanks."

"No problem. Thank for the autograph. Looking forward to seeing the next Storm."

"Might surprise you."

The young man reversed the truck and drove away. Chad paused at the door and hit Gregson's number. "Have you started undoing the rumors?"

"The studio doesn't want the news about Storm's being the victim of a murder attempt or that he hovers near death."

"Storm is dead. I have zero interest in Valerie. You can take care of that bit or you're

183

fired."

"Our contract has another three months. I'm holding you to that."

"Now hear this. I will not renew." Chad disconnected and refused to answer the return call. Let the rumor about the near death ride but if Gregson wouldn't take care of the Valerie mess, he would.

He opened the door to the house and headed to the kitchen. From the fridge he took a beer and sat at the island. He hit Emma's number and listened for her hello. He hoped she would speak to him. The call went to voice mail. He left a message and carried the beer to the bedroom where he showered and called again. Another voice mail.

As he dressed he turned on the TV for the noon broadcast of Hollywood Chatters. The latest clip of he and Valerie raised an angry roar. They spoke about the movie and alerted people to look for the hot tub scene. Not happening.

He hit Emma's number again and received the same response. He had to talk to her. He converted the time to east coast and called the office.

"The medical practice of Marshall and Grassi. The office is closed today. Who do you wish to speak to?"

He'd forgotten today was Saturday. "Emma Grassi."

"Sorry. She's on vacation. Is this an emergency?"

"Yes."

"I'll ring Dr. Marshall. Please hold."

Moments later he heard Manon's voice. "Chad Morgan here. I need to speak to Emma. She's not answering her calls."

"I know. She's on vacation. Goodbye."

"Don't hang up. I know about the rumors flying around. I've been on location with no reception for the past several weeks." He spoke so fast he wasn't sure she understood.

"Are you serious?"

"Yes. Please let Emma know I need to speak to her."

"I can't."

"What do you mean? Is she hurt? I'll fly out at once."

"Won't do you any good."

"Why not?"

"She's leaving on a cruise tomorrow. A singles' cruise. She boards ship in the morning from some hotel in Miami. I don't know which one. I don't even know if she took her phone."

"What's the name of the cruise line? Do you have any idea when tomorrow morning they leave?"

"I haven't a clue. Just the departure date . I think it's Caribbean Tours is the name of the line."

"Thanks."

"Just don't hurt her," Manon said.

"Not my objective." He disconnected and hit the computer to look up the cruise site. Moments later, he dialed a number. "I understand there's a cruise leaving from Miami

185

tomorrow. A singles' cruise."

"We do."

"Are there any cabins left?"

"There are several. One is a VIP suite."

"I would like to book that one."

The woman laughed. "Are you a VIP?"

"I could be. I want to book the cabin as a surprise for a woman who is taking the cruise."

"Your name?"

Chad drew a deep breath. Time to take the plunge. "Chad Morgan but I travel under the name Ian Greve."

"You're joking."

"Not at all. There are times when I want to go places under the radar. I've just finished a shoot and I want to spend some time with my girl."

"What name is Valerie traveling under?"

"Not her. This is the real deal and not Chatter gossip."

Moments later she spoke. "You're booked. Will you make the departure time?"

"When?"

"Eleven AM,"

"I'll be there. Another favor. Could you change Emma Grassi's room to the luxury suite and put me in hers."

"Done. Your information?"

Chad gave her the numbers. He hung up and scrambled to find a flight to Miami giving him time to take care of one little matter. He found one flight meeting his needs. The flight landed at nine forty-five AM giving him more than an hour to make the ship's departure time.

After hanging up he made a call to Hollywood Chatters. "Could you have time to interview Chad Morgan?"

"About you and Valerie?"

"Not a word about that. This is a real deal. Has to be this afternoon. I have a flight to catch."

She named a time. "Sounds good. I'll meet you at our studio."

He hung up, packed a suitcase, gathered all his documentation and hired a limo. After the interview he would have dinner and head to the airport.

* * *

When the phone on the night stand rang, Emma rolled on her side and reached for the receiver. "Hello."

The canned voice of the wake-up call sounded in her ear. She hung up, stretched and dashed to the bathroom. She'd slept for eight hours straight, something she hadn't done for months. After a shower, she dressed in the sundress she'd planned for the first day's cruise. She folded her travel clothes and packed them in the overnight bag. After leaving a tip for the maid, she rode the elevator to the ground floor and joined several of the women she'd met yesterday for breakfast.

She had just finished her second cup of coffee when an announcement filled the air.

"Passengers for the Caribbean Dream assemble in the lobby."

Emma followed the three women. She held her overnight bag and slung her purse over her shoulder. She and the women joined the large group of people onto the buses. A thrill of excitement bubbled through her. She might find someone to chase all thoughts of Chad away. She closed her eyes and allowed herself to dream.

At the dock she left the bus and walked up the gangplank. In her hand she held all the documents she needed. A pair of ship's officers stood at the head of the ramp. One took her papers and studied them and a list he held.

"You've been assigned to a different cabin. I believe you'll like the change."

"I hope my credit card will."

He laughed. "There will be no extra charge. Your new room is on Deck A. Use those stairs." He handed her the papers and a key card.

Emma followed the directions. At the cabin door, she used the card and entered. Her mouth gaped. Nor a room but a suite. A small sitting room opened into a bedroom and bath. A sliding door in the sitting room led to a balcony.

She noticed her suitcases had been set beside the bed. She lifted one and began unpacking. She glanced into the bathroom and saw a large shower, a sink and a commode. She placed the contents of her make-up case on the long counter where she saw a hair dryer, and a coffee set up. She returned to unpack her

188

clothes.

Quickly, she opened the dresser and loaded in her shorts, tops, sleepwear and underwear. As she hung dresses, she heard a click. Someone deposited a large suitcase on the sitting room carpet. She sucked in a breath. She'd known the room change had been a mistake. She left the suitcase and stepped into the other room.

Her eyes widened when she saw the intruder. "What are you doing here?" Chad's grin, the one that always turned her knees to rubber, flashed. She sank on the sofa.

"Do you really think I would let you sail away on a singles' cruise? I love you. I spent two weeks doing scenes in an area without cell phone reception. I knew nothing of the promo Gregson arranged with the aid of the Storm director." He pulled out his phone. "I want you to see this. Goes live tonight."

"A Hollywood Chatters exclusive. Chad Morgan, tell us your news."

"There's a new star in the Storm universe. Keep your eyes on Lightning. I'm off to new ventures."

"Are you saying you're retiring?"

"You'll have to watch the movie. But there's a new direction in my future.'

"Explain."

"A bad break in my left leg has made it necessary for me to wear this." He pulled up his pants' leg. "It won't be forever but until I can go without it, I'm making a slight change in my career. A new company has formed and the first movie we're making is Rob Grantlan's *Committee of Angels*. I'll be directing and starring in this medical suspense story."

"How can you take such a step?"

"I've been studying film making for years and have taken courses."

"Congratulations. When will the filming begin?"

"This fall but not until after I marry the woman I left behind. Her name is Emma Grassi and she's a nurse practitioner in private practice."

The clip ended. Chad slid his arm around her. "Will you marry me?"

She laughed. "After you announced your intentions of national TV what can I do but accept?"

"That's what I wanted to hear." He captured her mouth in a deep kiss.

The End

Books We Love Books by Janet Lane Walters

Visit Janet Lane Walters' BWl author page for purchase links

The Pisces Virgo Connection (Opposites in Love Book 6)

*The Leo – Aquarius Connection (*Opposites in Love Book 5*)*

The Cancer – Capricorn Connection (Opposites in Love Book 4)

The Gemini – Sagittarius Connection (Opposites in Love Book 3)

The Taurus – Scorpio Connection (Opposites in Love Book 2)

The Aries – Libra Connection (Opposites in Love Book 1)

Seducing The Nurse

Discovering the Jewels' Secret

Confronting the Wizards

Search for the White Jewel

Murder and Herbal Tea (A Katherine Miller Mystery)

Murder and Bitter Tea (A Katherine Miller Mystery)

Murder and Tainted Tea (A Katherine Miller Mystery)

Murder and Poisonous Tea (A Katherine Miller Mystery)

Young Adult books By J L Walters

Escape (Affinities Book 1 - Young Adult
Fantasy)
Havens (Affinities Book 2 - Young Adult
fantasy, Books We Love)
Searches (Affinities Book 3 - Young Adult
Fantasy, Books We Love)
Confrontations (Affinities)

Janet Lane Walters was born in
Wilkensburg, Pennsylvania on July 17, 1936,
reported to be the hottest day of the summer.
She has been a published author since 1968,
beginning with short stories and moving into
novels when an editor told her a short story
sounded like a synopsis for a novel. In the 1970s
and 1980s she published four sweet nurse

romance novels. Then she returned to school to earn a BS in Nursing and a BA in English. Returning to work as a nurse to help put four children through college, she put her writing career on hold. In 1993 she retired from nursing and began writing again. A new nurse romance followed in print. Then she discovered electronic publishing and since 1998 has been electronically published.

Janet calls herself an eclectic writer since she moves from genre to genre. There are mysteries featuring Katherine Miller, a former nurse who seems to stumble over bodies wherever she goes. Using her interest in Astrology, she has several series that use Astrology as a premise for the stories. Once she earned enough money to travel to Ireland by casting charts for people. She has many books in the romance genre, some of them contemporary and nurse romance, while others fall into the fantasy or paranormal categories of romance. She is keenly interested in reincarnation and has used this as a jumping point for at least two novels. Two of her novels deal with alternate worlds using a love affair with Ancient Egypt.

Under her other name, J.L. Walters, she has written a YA fantasy series called Affinities. She has also written a non-fiction book with co-author Jane Toombs that won the EPIC Award in 2003 for best Non-fiction. During her career she has received other awards and has a number of great reviews.

Besides her four adult children, she has seven grandchildren. Five of them are the models for the YA series. The other two arrived too late to play a large role in the series. Four of her grandchildren are bi-racial and three are Chinese so the eclectic even invades her family. She has been married to the same man for more than 50 years. He's a psychiatrist who refuses to cure her obsession for writing.